Pregnant to my Dad's Best-Friend

Axel and Chastity book 2

Lexie Miers

Chapter 1

Chastity

AFTER A POST-COITAL NAP, AXEL CONVINCED ME TO ABANDON MY studies and go and see the apartment he'd purchased in the area.

"I can't believe you actually bought an apartment here," I said, shaking my head as I climbed into his car. "That's so extreme."

He turned the key and started the engine on his ridiculously expensive sports car. "I wanted to be close to you."

I crossed my arms over my chest and stared at him. "Stalker."

He laughed, and the sound filled the cabin of the car, the most incredible sound on the planet.

I couldn't help but smile, happiness pouring through me.

"So, it was a bit much, huh?" he asked, driving through the streets towards town.

I glanced out the window. "Well, it was kind of a grand gesture. I can't fault you there."

I looked back at him, my chest tightening. "But what if I'd said no?"

"You mean to us getting back together?"

I nodded. "Yeah. What would you have done?"

He shrugged. "Signed the place over to you, dropped off the keys, and taken my broken ass home again."

My mouth dropped open. "You would have given me an apartment? Just like that?"

Axel turned down another street then glanced at me. "Yeah, of course."

I didn't believe it. How could anyone just give away something so valuable? My own mother had worked her fingers to the bone to provide a roof over my head.

I stared out the window, a swirl of emotions clogging up my chest and throat.

"Hey, hey… what's going on inside your head?" Axel asked, sliding a hand over my thigh.

I looked down at my leg and stared at the way he possessively caressed the skin there.

I'd missed his touch. So much.

Taking a deep breath, I tried to calm the panic. "Nothing. I just can't really comprehend having that much money. My parents, my mom in particular, struggled to pay the mortgage. The utilities. Food. And you would just… give me an apartment."

Axel pulled into a parking lot just off the street and shut off the engine.

"Why'd you stop?" I asked.

He turned in the seat and grinned at me. "Because we're here."

"Whoa, that really was just five minutes." I glanced around. It was a nice neighborhood, but I didn't really recognize it.

"Hey, listen to me for a sec, okay?" he soothed, squeezing my thigh a little.

I turned around to face him, his tone telling me he was about to get all serious on me.

"Okay. I'm listening."

"I say this without vanity, but I have a lot of money."

I laughed at him. "Oh, yeah, you sound incredibly modest."

He sighed. "I have a point, so listen to me, okay?"

I crossed my arms over my chest, uncomfortable with this conversation but nodded, nonetheless. "I'm listening, go on."

He took a deep breath then exhaled slowly. "I grew up wealthy. My parents sent me to the best schools, got me everything I wanted, then ignored the fact that I existed."

I reached across the car and squeezed his hand, hating that he'd had such a crappy childhood.

"It's okay, because after they'd paid for me to go to college, they basically cut me off to prove that I couldn't survive without them."

I grinned at him, already knowing where this story was going. "But you did."

"Of course, I did. I made sure of it. I got a good job then started my own company, and have been pushing hard ever since."

"It makes sense," I agreed, smiling at him. "You wanted to prove you could do it on your own."

"I did, and I still was—until I met you. Now I'm looking into taking on some partners, downsizing maybe. Selling off the business or just delegating some of my roles. I'm not sure yet, but you've inspired me to change my life."

I huffed out a laugh. "Ah… I don't understand. I've made you want to stop working?"

Was that a compliment?

He sighed. "I'm not explaining this right. I don't want to just accumulate wealth for the sake of it anymore, Chastity. I want it to mean something more. I want the money to give us a better life. That's the point of money, right?"

I nodded, still not seeing the big picture yet. "Sure." It came out more like a question.

He ran a hand through his hair and sighed. "Look, all I meant by this is that is…" He groaned then looked me straight in the eye. "Money means nothing to me if I can't have you. So… if you didn't want me, then the apartment, the money I had to buy it, and the car, all mean nothing."

I leaned over and kissed him.

He was going around in a circle, and instead of listening to the words, I heard the intent behind them.

Pulling back, I looked into his eyes. "I love you too."

He smiled at me. "How are you already smarter than me?"

I laughed. "Hardly! But it's nice that you think I'm smart. So, are you going to show me this apartment?"

"Let's go," he said, and jumped out of the car.

I followed suit and looked around. "Nice area."

There were a few cafés and restaurants as well as random shops along the opposite side of the street, facing the modern looking apartment building that was apparently our destination.

"I thought it would be good to be close to some amenities. The place has a gym for me, a laundry service if we both just want to chill." He took my hand and led me into a huge building that was far flashier on the inside than it looked on the outside.

It had marble floors and a concierge waiting at the desk. "Can I help you, sir?"

Axel nodded. "Yes and no. I'm Axel Patterson and I purchased the penthouse here last week. The closing was a few days ago and I have the keys, so I'd like to take a look now. Do you have any access cards that I need?"

The concierge's eyes widened. "It's nice to meet you, sir. I'm Tony. Let me get the building forms out for you and I'll set you up with everything you need."

"Chastity's name needs to be on everything as well," Axel said, indicating to me. "She goes to school nearby and will probably use this place more than I do."

"Of course, sir," Tony said. "I'll just get your daughter to sign the papers too."

I laughed out loud, then looked at the guy behind the desk. "I'm not his daughter, Tony."

The guy stared at me, frozen with shock.

I put my hand on the desk and grinned at him. I couldn't believe he'd actually said it, and a streak of cheekiness took over. "I mean… I understand your confusion and technically, he could be. The age gap between us is twenty years. But, nope. Not us."

Axel glared at the concierge, steam practically rising from his ears. "She's my girlfriend, and I suggest you give her the respect that deserves."

Tony sputtered out an apology and I turned away so he didn't see me grin and struggle not to laugh again. It was the first time someone had assumed I was Axel's daughter, and I was pretty sure it wouldn't be the last. We had to keep a sense of humor about it, surely?

Within ten minutes we'd both signed all the relevant paperwork and were being personally escorted up the elevator by the concierge.

"If you need anything from me at all, please don't hesitate to call."

"You can go, Tony," Axel said, flicking his hand to dismiss the poor guy.

I smiled at him as he shut the door, then raced over to the windows that faced the ocean, only a few blocks away. "Oh my God, Axel, this view is incredible."

I pressed a hand to the cool glass and stared out. Wow.

Axel dropped the keys on the kitchen counter behind me and I whirled around, still sensing his displeasure.

"What's the matter, Daddy?" I asked him, grinning as widely as I could. "Don't you want people to think I'm your little girl?"

He thrust his hands into his jean pockets and glowered at me. He looked as sexy as sin, and I marveled at the fact the concierge had mistaken him for anything more than my boyfriend. He looked thirty, thirty-five, tops.

"No. I don't want that," he growled.

I pouted and dropped to my knees, crawling over the plush carpet and staring up at him. I wanted him again, and I had to assume that the best way to get him out of this mood was to prove to him how young and virile he really was.

He stared down at me as I approached, then got up on my knees right in front of him.

"This carpet is incredible," I said as I reached for the button on his jeans. "You'll have to give me the grand tour. In a moment."

"In a moment, huh?" he asked, sliding his hand around the back of my head, his eyes darkening with desire.

"Yeah..." I nodded, opening the zipper and taking out his cock. "Later."

I took the head into my mouth, loving the way his groan filled the air around me. I was so much more confident doing this now.

I moved my hand on the shaft, enjoying the way his flesh got larger and hotter against my palm.

His taste was so special. Like macadamia nut oil, but hot and sexy. It was so distinctly him, and I loved it. All of it.

Then he was tugging me to my feet and grabbing me up in his arms.

He twirled me around, set me on the kitchen counter and kissed me hungrily.

He lifted my skirt, found my underwear, and tore our mouths apart so he could drag my undies off and down my legs.

When he came back, I opened my thighs willingly. He was grunting and moving with quick, jerky motions. He wanted me, and he didn't care about finesse and concern. This was about passion and need. And imprinting himself all over me.

He grabbed my ass and dragged me to the edge of the counter. I gasped at the move as the cold marble pressed into my behind. But then he was there, hot and insistent against me.

I lifted my chin and he kissed me, his tongue piercing my lips as his cock pressed into my softness. The hard, mushroomed head of his opened me, and I threw my head back, gasping at the pressure.

It was so fast, so powerful. A sob rose in my throat at how right it felt to be with this man in my arms. He set his teeth to my neck and sucked the skin there, marking me. Again.

He thrust all the way to the hilt, and I moaned at the feeling of fullness.

"You okay?" he whispered, and I closed my eyes on the wave of love that flowed over me.

"Yes," I reassured him, not wanting to break the spell cast over us. "Don't stop."

And he didn't. He pulled back then thrust forward into me, again and again.

I gasped and moaned, clinging to him as he relentlessly fucked me into the kitchen counter hot and fast, the sounds of our slapping flesh and groans filled the white kitchen. Suddenly he groaned and pulled out, spilling his heat all over me while he plundered my mouth for a final kiss.

When he pulled back from the kiss, he was panting and pressed his forehead against mine. I closed my eyes and held him tightly against me, reveling in the feeling that came from bringing him to such a state of pleasure.

"I'm sorry." He panted. "I couldn't control it."

I laughed and lifted my head, smiling up at me. "Never apologize for fucking me. Never."

Axel bent his head and kissed my lips. "We've gotta get you on the pill."

I groaned and glanced down at my new top, now covered in cum. "Yeah… or invest in a new wardrobe."

We laughed as we raced to the new shower to clean up. He'd remembered to pull out of me this time, but before at the dorm?

He hadn't.

Chapter 2

Axel

I TUGGED MY JEANS BACK ON AND GRIMACED AT THE FEEL OF THEM against my clean skin. "We need some new clothes."

Chastity chuckled as she stood wearing only her underwear, staring down at the soiled top and skirt on the floor. "Well, I certainly do."

Heat flushed up my cheeks. "Ah… yeah. Sorry about that. Let me make a phone call and I'll get you some new things. What size are you? A six?"

"Ha!" she said, crossing her arms over her ample breasts. "More like an eight or ten."

I kissed her lips and stepped away, grabbing for my phone. "Give me a sec."

A cheery Tony picked up when I called the front desk. "Concierge speaking."

"Tony, it's Axel from the penthouse."

"Oh, sir! I wanted to apologize again for my blunder."

"You can make it up to us by sending someone out to do some shopping. We both need some new clothes. Jeans, a couple of tops. Put it on my bill."

"Of course, sir. I'll get someone to watch the desk, then go myself. Can you give me your sizes and some color options?"

I did, then hung up the phone.

Chastity came up next to me, sliding her small hand into mine. "Are you going to show me the apartment now?"

I looked down at her, loving the soft look of contentment in her eyes. "Sure. But it'll be the first time for me too, so I'm not sure I can give you much of a tour."

Her eyebrows climbed high on her forehead. "What do you mean?"

I shrugged. "Exactly what I said. I bought this place, sight unseen. So, let's go see it together."

"You—"

I grabbed Chastity's hand and dragged her to the front door. Buying a penthouse apartment in a great area wasn't a financial risk as far as I was concerned. It was furnished and had been styled by an interior decorator. It would be an easy piece of real estate to sell once we were done with it.

"Let's start at the front door," I said, dragging her back to the front door, then turning her around to face the apartment. "So, this is the apartment I bought."

I waved my hand around, and she giggled. She was standing in her underwear, looking utterly gorgeous.

"It's very nice," she said. "Where's the bedroom?"

I groaned and tapped her gently on her round ass. "Let's go see, shall we?"

We turned left, down the hall and stepped into the first room. The master suite. "I think we found it."

"Oh... I like it!" she said, running her hand over the blue and black patterned comforter, then sticking her head in the ensuite bathroom. "It has a bathtub and the biggest shower. Come see!"

I grinned as I walked after her, loving her enthusiasm.

"Next time, we'll look at apartments together and choose one we both like."

She twisted around and wrapped her arms around my neck. "I love this one. The view is amazing. The bedroom is huge, and I'm going to love soaking in that tub."

Tick, tick, tick. I do know her!

"I'm glad you like it," I said, kissing her soft lips and sliding my hands around her tiny waist. "Once we get some clothes, how about we go out for some early dinner then come back and I give you that orgasm I owe you?"

Her eyes widened as her eyebrows shot up. "You don't owe me anything."

"Oh, but I do," I said. "And I will love giving it to you."

She bit her lip, her cheeks coloring a beautiful rose. "Dinner sounds great, but how long are you staying? Should I go back to school to pick up some stuff? Or are you heading home soon?"

It was Saturday afternoon, and I had several important meetings on Monday. "I'll stay until tomorrow afternoon, but then I'll really need to head back to the city."

She kissed me again. "Okay, perfect. So, we can just chill together tonight and tomorrow. Then you'll drop me back?"

I nodded. "Of course. I have to introduce you to your car, too."

"Ooohhh." She grinned, and I held her hand as we walked around the rest of the apartment. There were three bedrooms, a huge kitchen and living area, and two bathrooms.

"Can I invite my parents to stay here one weekend?" she asked when we'd finished the tour and she was looking through the kitchen cabinets for a glass to get some water.

"Ah... yeah. Of course," I responded, though I hadn't really thought about anyone using it except us. "Or if you have any friends you want to come stay, that would be fine too. It's three bedrooms. We can still make a whole lot of racket at one end if they're sleeping down the other end of the apartment."

Chastity slapped her hand over her mouth, her eyes bulging. "I still can't believe Dad walked in on us. He hasn't really spoken to me since that day."

I inhaled sharply. "It would have been a bit of a shock."

And one I really couldn't empathize with. I didn't have kids. Speaking of which… "How do you feel about going on the pill?"

She drank a sip of water, then tilted her head. "Is that what you normally do with your girlfriends?"

I laughed out loud at that one. "Uh… no. I don't have girlfriends, and normally a woman's choices regarding her body are totally up to her."

Chastity pressed her lips together and squinted at me. "Normally? I'm really not understanding."

I pressed my hands into the marble countertop and groaned. "I can't control myself with you. In my past, those women were experienced. They carried protection, and so did I. The encounters were calculated. But with you, I can't stop myself. I want to feel your naked pussy wrapped around my cock. It's just…"

I growled because I couldn't quite put into words how little control I had around her. She was so sweet, and yet as seductive as Helen of Troy. I didn't want latex between us. I didn't want anything between us. I wanted to be able to take her anywhere, any time.

She slapped her hands to her cheeks and closed her eyes. "Oh my God," she whispered. "I can't believe you talk like that."

I stared at her, noticing the way her chest rose and fell as though she were excited.

"Unless you want to get pregnant?" I asked her. "Because that would change everything."

And I would not complain. A baby with the woman I loved? What better way to enjoy our new life?

Chastity dropped her hands down and smiled at me. "I love the fact you want that. It's amazing. But I have so many things I want to do first. I've never even left the state. I haven't traveled…"

"Oh, then we need to do that." I said, ideas flooding my mind. "Paris. Spain. London."

She laughed at me. "Disneyworld. Canada. Vegas!"

"When's your birthday?" I asked, realizing I didn't know, which was sad considering I'd just offered her a baby.

"It's next week, actually. January the tenth."

"Perfect! Let's go to Vegas."

Her eyes went wide and suspiciously shiny. "Seriously? Just like that?"

"Yes, Let's go and do Vegas properly. Lots of gambling, shows, and drinking."

She walked over to me and slid her hands up my torso. "Axel, that would be amazing. Thank you."

I bent my head to kiss her, then heard the knock at the door.

I groaned. "Fucking interruptions."

She giggled. "That's probably Tony with our clothes."

I glanced down at her cleavage pushed up by her white bra. "I prefer you undressed."

She raised an eyebrow. "And the people in the restaurant at dinner?"

I pulled out of her arms. "No. They don't get to see you like this."

She waved her hand at me. "Then go grab the clothes, and I'll meet you in the bedroom."

She flounced away and I watched her luscious ass flex as she moved.

Grrr... I could take her right now.

Another knock at the door sounded. "Coming!"

I stomped toward the entry wearing only jeans and wrenched open the door.

"Oh. Sir. I brought…"

I extended my arm to Tony, who was standing at the door laden down with suit bags and retail bags. "Come on in."

Tony hurried forward. "May I put these in the bedroom?"

"No. Chastity is in there. Just set everything on the sofa."

He'd bought a lot from what I could tell. He was carrying at least eight shopping bags, and long suit bags obviously containing something for me.

"There you go, sir," he said, heading towards the door.

"Thanks, Tony." I waved him out. "Just lock the door behind you. Thanks."

As soon as the door had shut, Chastity walked out, all gorgeous suntanned flesh on display. "When are you going to forgive him?"

I shrugged. "No idea. Maybe next year."

I lifted up a bright pink bag. "I think some of these are for you."

"Oohhh." Chastity dropped to her knees, and I watched her go through the bags with gasps of delight and squeals of glee. "This is better than Christmas."

I sat on the sofa and watched her as she unpacked everything and began to try the clothes on. This was how Christmas should have been. Us nearly naked, having just had sex. Presents everywhere, and Chastity as happy as a clam.

Next Christmas I'd make sure we were together for the whole day, whether she wanted to do her normal lunch and dinner routine with her parents, or I whisked her off to Paris for the week.

Either way worked for me. Now that I had this delightful girl back in my life, I was never letting her go again.

Chapter 3

Chastity

I grabbed Axel's face for one final kiss and hugged him tightly to me. We'd have an amazing night together. I'd worn my new black dress Tony the concierge purchased for me, and we'd had a lovely dinner.

Afterwards, we'd gone for a walk, eaten ice cream and made love all through the night. This morning he'd taken me out for a late brunch, and we'd laughed and chatted like we'd been together forever.

Axel hadn't stopped touching me or kissing me, and no one who was looking at us would ever have mistaken us for father and daughter.

But the weekend was almost over, and Axel had a two-hour drive ahead of him.

"I don't want you to go." I pouted, clinging tightly to his hands. He was dropping me off at the front gate, and I didn't want to go back to school without him.

He chuckled, raised my hands up and kissed my knuckles. "Trust me, beautiful. If I could stay, I would."

I sighed. "Yeah, and I suppose I have to get back too. Classes. Studying. Stuff."

Everything my life had been before I'd met him.

He pulled back and grinned down at me. "Don't forget to check out your car. I had it put in the dorm's parking lot, out the back. Keys are in your room."

"Which one is it?" I asked. "There's hundreds of cars out there."

He winked. "You'll know which one it is, trust me. And if you can't work it out, just call me and I'll tell you what to look for."

Ooooh... a mystery! And a surprise!

"Axel, you spoil me too much." And I really didn't feel like I deserved it.

"Hardly," he said, walking back to his car. "Wait until you've been with me for a year or two. By then I should have spoiled you sufficiently."

He opened the door to his car and turned back to grin at me.

"Two years?" I asked, staring at him in awe. "What do you mean?"

"Well, I need to fly you all over the world first, make love to you in every major city on the planet. Buy you clothes, and jewelry and anything else your heart desires."

A lump of emotion caught in my throat. "You've already bought me jewelry and clothes, and you are everything my heart desires."

Axel ran back to me and swept me up in his arms, groaning as he hugged me tightly. "*That* is why I love you. You really don't want me for my money, do you?"

I pulled back and glared up at him. "Are you honestly asking me that? Of course not! Look... I love that you're successful and smart and you work so hard. That makes me admire you. But I grew up with very little money, and I intend to make my own. So, no, I'm not with you for your money."

He kissed me hard and fast on the lips, then pulled away. "Thank you."

"Now," I said, giving his broad chest a shove. "Go make more millions, Daddy Warbucks."

He mock scowled at me, and I laughed, wrapping my arms around my body. "Bye."

I watched him drive away, my heart beating a dancing type tempo in my chest.

When he'd driven away and I could no longer see him, I squealed, unable to keep it in any longer. We were back together! And my dad approved of us.

I wasn't really sure how Axel had pulled that off, but he had.

My cell phone rang, and I pulled it out of my pocket.

A huge grin split my face as I answered, "Miss me already?"

Axel chuckled. "Oh, yeah. Definitely. But I wanted to ask you one more thing."

"Yeah?"

"Can you call your dad? I think he wants to talk to you."

I laughed. "That is seriously freaky mind reading. I was just thinking about you and Dad, and wondering how you really convinced him we were okay."

"I just told him the truth, beautiful. About how much I love you, and he knows me well enough to know that's never been me before, which makes you special."

I gulped. I wasn't sure I'd ever get sick of hearing him say things like that. "Um... thank you for telling me that again. I kinda love hearing it."

"Good. Because it's the truth. But I think Pat misses you."

My breath hitched in my throat. "Yeah, I didn't really say goodbye to him."

And considering that Dad was one of the main factors of why I was looking forward to going home this holiday season, that said a lot about how much our relationship had deteriorated.

"Well, the apartment's there if your parents need a place to stay, and you have your car too, whenever you want to drive back to see us."

I closed my eyes for a brief moment and sent a prayer of thanks up to the sky. "Thank you, Axel. Really. That sort of freedom is mind blowing to me."

"Go see your car and send me a photo of you in it."

I laughed, turning on the ball of my foot to walk in the direction of my dorm room. "Going to get the keys now."

"Okay, beautiful. Chat soon."

He hung up and I slid my cell phone into my pocket and ran all the way back to my room. The keys were still sitting where I'd left them, and I snatched them up.

"What sort of car are you?" I asked the silver key, staring down at the fob attached to it.

I froze. "No way."

I raced out of my room, down the hallway, and almost knocked over another girl in my haste. "Sorry!" I yelled as I kept running.

"Oh my God!" I passed through the door that led into the parking lot and glanced around. Left. Right. "Oh my God."

There it was.

A bright blue VW Beetle. And from the looks of it, brand new.

I slapped my hands over my mouth to stop the scream that rose in my throat.

I crept closer, staring and gaping. There was a huge red bow stuck to the hood and I had to gulp back the tears that threatened my composure.

"It's beautiful."

My phone dinged, and I lifted it up.

"Do you like it?"

I twisted around, set my phone to selfie mode, and took a pic of me grinning, tears in my eyes and the car in the background.

I sent him the photo and added text. **You made me cry. I'm so overwhelmed. Thank you.**

I lifted the keys and pressed the button, part of me expecting it to not work. There was no way this was my car.

But the lights flashed and when I walked over, the door was unlocked.

I got a message straight back. **One of many gifts you'll be getting, so prepare to be spoiled.**

I squealed, sounding juvenile when I did, then I hoped in the driver's seat, with nowhere to go. It was beautiful. So new it smelled amazing, but strange at the same time.

I ran my hand over the leather steering wheel and stared down at all the buttons on the dashboard. I had no idea how to work any of this, but I was sure I could figure it out.

Picking up my phone, I took a few more photos then flicked to my address book. Time to call Dad.

He picked up on the second ring. "Chastity."

"Hey, Dad."

My gut was tight with tension, wondering what he would say next.

"I missed not having you here for New Year's."

I smiled. I didn't usually spend New Year's Eve with my dad, but I got his meaning.

"Yeah… I wish I'd been there too. I hope you understood why I left."

"I did. Breaking up is hard."

I nodded, though he couldn't see me. "Yeah, it was. My first break-up, actually."

"Have you heard from Axel since then?" he asked, the tone of his voice higher than normal, like he was anxious.

"Yeah, he came by school yesterday actually."

"He came by?" Dad repeated. "How?"

I laughed. "What do you mean, how? He drove. Came into the college grounds, found me at the library, but the librarian refused to let him in, so she made him wait outside."

My dad laughed. "Axel was refused entry into a library? Oh, I would have liked to be there to see that."

I grinned. "Yeah, it was sort of awesome."

There was a long beat of silence, then he asked, "So… what happened?"

My chest squeezed tight, and my breath caught in my throat. "Well… we got back together."

Silence.

"Dad?"

"I'm here. Did you two sort everything out?"

"Yeah, we did. As much as we could. I was worried about you and how you felt about everything. But Axel said you gave him permission to come and apologize."

I bit my lip, inhaling deeply through my nose. I hadn't realized talking to my father about this stuff would be so difficult.

"I did. And I'm glad he apologized for being a dick. Tell me… how does a billionaire say I'm sorry? I've never heard those words cross Axel's lips."

"Well," I smiled at the memory. "He did say he was sorry, multiple times. And he bought me some things to make us dating each other easier. You know, with the whole long-distance thing."

"What kind of things did he buy you?"

"Well, he got me a car."

"A car! What kind?"

"A Beetle."

I could almost hear my dad's teeth gnashing together.

"What else?"

"Well, the second thing isn't for me, so to speak…" Though he would have given it to me if we'd broken up. Something I still found to be an utterly ridiculous concept. "But he bought an apartment about five minutes from here, so he can stay when he comes for weekends. And he said you or Mom, can come stay too. It's three bedrooms."

More silence, with a little bit of teeth cracking on the other end of the line.

"Dad? You okay?"

"Just be careful, baby, okay? I love Axel, but his track record with dating is shit. He's not good boyfriend material, and I want only good things for you."

My stomach dropped. "I know, Dad. Thank you. And I'm really sorry about everything."

"You mean about dating my best friend behind my back and lying to me?"

Gulp. Fuck.

"Yeah. All of that, Dad. I'm so sorry."

God, it took a lot for me to say it. I wasn't sorry for dating Axel, but I was extremely sorry for hurting my father. So, I was sucking it up and being accountable.

"I know, baby. Okay." He took a big breath, then blew it out in a sigh. "Thank you for telling me you two are back together."

"No problem."

My stomach churned and I put a hand on my belly to stop the feelings from rising too high.

"I better go, Chastity. We'll talk during the week, okay?"

"Sure! Thanks, Dad."

He hung up and I closed my eyes on a wave of pain. I'd known this moment was coming. Debt collection, for all the sneaking around I'd done.

I opened my eyes, got out of my new car, and locked it. I'd send Mom a few pics and show her my new gift, though just like my dad, I was pretty sure she wouldn't be happy to hear about it.

Chapter 4

Chastity

And guess what? I was right. My mother wasn't happy at all about the photos I sent her. She was actually pretty pissed off that I'd gotten a new car, while she still drove around in something nearly twenty years old.

I tried to backtrack and apologize, for what, I wasn't sure. Having a rich boyfriend, maybe? Either way, I went into my final semester with a heavy heart and a mix of emotions.

Schoolwork was difficult and my life seemed lacklustre without Axel's presence. But he messaged me all the time and we chatted every night. When Friday finally rolled around, I couldn't wait to get out of the place.

"Hey, I was thinking of coming back home this weekend," I said to him on Friday around lunchtime. He'd called me on one of his rare breaks. "Are you going to be around?"

"Of course, I'll be around," he said, sounding extremely enthusiastic. Then he hissed, "Shit. I've got a ton work to do on Sunday, and a business dinner Saturday night."

I bit my lip, sadness welling up inside of me. "Can I come to the dinner? Or would I be totally out of place?"

I hated inviting myself. Talk about rude, but I wanted him to know that I'd fit into his life however I could.

"You'd like to do that?" he asked quietly. "Come with me to one of my boring work dinners?"

"Yes! Of course, I would. But only if that would suit you. I don't want to sit there all alone because you're talking to some foreign guy I've never met."

Axel laughed. "No, actually, these business dinners are social events. My board of directors bring their wives. I just… I've never had one to take."

I inhaled sharply, those words twanging at my heart strings. "Well, we're not married, but I'd love to go if you're okay with that."

"I would love it," he said.

"Then it's a date." I grinned, feeling excited for the first time all week. "I can drive home tonight, maybe catch up with Mom for a bit, then come over?"

"I've gotta work late tonight," he said, though I could hear the regret in his voice. "But how about I pick you up for lunch on Saturday and we spend the day together? Then do dinner, sleep together, then Sunday, I'll need to get working again."

Lunch, dinner, a night, and most of Saturday? I'd take it.

"Sounds perfect. And I'm sure my parents will want to see me."

There was a beat of silence. "Did you call Patrick?"

"Yeah, I did." And his opinion of Axel still worried me.

"Good. So, you're both okay?"

I bit my lip and mulled it over for a moment. "Yeah, I think so. Although, if you need to work Sunday, maybe I'll invite him for lunch or something. Might be good to see him. Clear the air."

"Great idea, beautiful. Now I've gotta go. But I'll see you tomorrow, yeah?"

"Yes!" I repeated, jumping up from my chair and grabbing my bag. "I've got one more class, then I'll hit the road. My first trip in the new car."

He chuckled. "Enjoy. I'll see you soon."

"Bye."

He hung up, and I jumped a little. I was going home in my new car, and I was going to see Axel again. There couldn't be a better way to spend a weekend.

My last class finished, I raced back to my room to pack. I had some clothes at my mom's house, but I still needed a few things.

"Where you going?" Hope, my roommate, asked as I hurried in. "I thought you were sticking around this weekend."

I grinned at her. She just wanted a study partner. "Not anymore. My boyfriend wants me to go to a business dinner with him, and I thought I could take my new car for a spin."

Hope glowed green with envy. "Yeah, I get that. It's so nice in those first few months of a relationship, isn't it? The honeymoon phase is the best."

I grabbed my suitcase and began packing clothes. Panties and bras, leggings and jeans. Which dress was I going to wear tomorrow night? The black one the concierge purchased or was there a better choice?

If this was going to become a regular thing, I was definitely going to need some new clothes. Some dressier ones.

"Honeymoon phase?" I repeated, reaching for some textbooks I could read in any down time.

"Yeah," Hope said, sitting on her bed and pulling her legs up so she could sit cross-legged. "You know—the first three months is when everything's awesome. Your partner's perfect. He says all the right things, the sex is amazing. Then after that, things start to annoy you. The sex goes downhill, and you start to fight."

Hope pouted as though she were remembering so many fights, and break-ups, it tugged at my heart.

"Well, this is my first relationship," I said, closing the zipper on my suitcase. "And he's twice my age and dated more women than I can count. So, hopefully between us, we can find our way through the jungle together."

I'd been really worried about the long-distance thing, but if this was how it was going to be—weekends together, and planning trips like Vegas next week—then we'd make it. No problem.

"Is he really twice your age?" Hope asked, her eyebrows flicking up on her forehead. "Like… actually, double?"

I shrugged. "Pretty much."

I was twenty-one, almost twenty-two. And Axel was forty-one.

Hope's mouth dropped open, and she stared at me like I was crazy. "Then he's old! Why would you want to date someone like that? Unless he's rich and you're with him for his money or something?"

I glared at her. "Excuse me?"

"I'm just saying—"

"You're saying I've either got Daddy issues or I'm a gold digger." I shoved the suitcase onto the ground and snatched up my phone. "Axel is sweet and sexy and successful. And if you want a concrete reason for why I'm with him…"

I flipped to the few photos I had of him, then found the one of him standing in nothing but a towel. His hair was still wet from the shower, and he had a smile on his face that melted my heart. But the reason I chose it was because every muscle in his arms and chest was so clearly defined. He was fucking delicious.

I turned the phone around and walked it over to her bed.

"That's him?" she asked, taking the phone.

"Yes," I ground out, my temper getting the better of me. "And just so you know, he's got money. He bought me my new car. But that's not why I'm with him. It's because he's seriously amazing in bed."

I snatched my phone back from the jealous chick that I used to consider a friend and grabbed my bag. "See you on Monday."

Then I walked out the door, muttering to myself.

"What is wrong with everyone?" I groaned, taking my keys out and swinging them around my fingers while I walked to the car. "Mom's shitty to me, Dad thinks Axel's an asshole. Now Hope is making me feel like crap, too."

I walked out into the parking lot and found my new little car. The usual happiness I felt in seeing it was gone. If I went to visit either of my parents, they'd grump about the car or Axel, and I really wasn't up for that. So, what were my options this weekend?

The apartment? Did I really want to be alone? My mom's? I groaned at the possibility of dealing with her.

Getting in the car after tossing my suitcase in the backseat, I started the engine and pulled out of the lot. My mind in a jumble, I just started driving, mulling over each of the places I should go. Mom would be happy to see me, but would she turn my newly ignited relationship against me? Probably.

Did I want to deal with that tonight? Nope.

Dad? He might have plans this weekend. After all, he was a young, single guy, much like Axel had been. He'd have plans up the wazoo. But then again, I would love to see his face when I told him I was going to a work thing with Axel.

A lightness filled my heart as I drove past the apartment Axel had bought for us to spend time together and kept on driving home.

I glanced at the fuel gauge, making sure I had enough gas to get all the way to my Dad's place, assuming he wanted me to stay with him last minute. Otherwise, I'd have to just ask Axel if I could crash at his condo two nights in a row.

That would probably test our relationship since he'd said he couldn't do tonight.

I clicked my cell phone into Bluetooth speaker mode and called my dad.

He picked up right away. "Hey, sweetheart. This is a surprise."

"Hey, Dad! Yeah... well, I have another surprise. I'm driving down this weekend and was wondering if I could crash at your place tonight? No stress if you have plans to go out, I'll just study and get an early night."

"Ah... yeah. Okay, sure!"

"It's okay if you can't, Dad. I'll figure something out."

"No!" He said, a little more forcefully than I'd expected. "I want to see you, and you can come. I already had dinner plans, so if you're okay for me to go out for a couple of hours..."

"Yeah, of course I am. I have a ton of studying to do."

"Then, if you don't mind me asking, how come the surprise trip if you have a lot of work to do?"

I inhaled sharply, guarding my heart against the possible backlash I was about to receive. "Axel has a work dinner tomorrow night and asked me to join him. And since we didn't really get to say goodbye properly last week, I thought we could spend tonight together and go out for breakfast, maybe?"

I held my breath and waited.

When my father spoke, his voice was a little higher and quieter than I expected. "A work dinner? You're going to a-a work dinner with him?"

I grinned and tried not to laugh out loud. "Yeah. Why? Is that bad?"

"Oh, no," Dad reassured me. "It's not that. Just… don't worry about it. I'll see you when you get here. You've got your key, right?"

"I do."

"Well, I'll see you at home. There's food in the fridge and some cash in the fruit bowl if you want to order something in."

Love filled my heart. "Thanks, Dad."

"See you soon."

He hung up and I let the giggle escape. "Well, that was a step in the right direction."

Glancing at the dashboard, I realized I wasn't going to get to Dad's until about six pm, and that was assuming the traffic wasn't terrible. I might miss seeing him before he went out, but that was okay. There was plenty of time to catch up with him before tomorrow.

Chapter 5

Chastity

As it happened, the traffic was terrible.

I got to Dad's closer to seven pm, than six. Something I made a note of for future travel. Friday traffic was shit! I parked on the street, grabbed my bags, and carried everything up to my dad's apartment. The place was clean and quiet, and exactly what I needed after a stressful week of school.

I heated up some leftover chicken I found in the fridge, made a salad, and sat down in front of the tv to watch some Netflix. When my phone went off, I picked it up with my mouth full. "Hmm… h'lllo."

"Hey, beautiful. Did you make it down okay?" Axel's deep voice vibrated down the phone line and happiness filled my heart.

"Hey!" I said, putting my plate down and swallowing what was still in my mouth. "Yeah, I did. But for future reference, Friday night traffic sucks."

He chuckled. "Yeah, it does. Probably not something you've had to deal with before."

"Especially not as the driver," I agreed. As the passenger, I rarely noticed traffic patterns, but that was about to change. "Next time, unless we have something happening, I think I'll come down on Saturday morning."

"Sounds good," he said, and his voice was all soft and warm. Honey-like.

"You seem happy," I said, grinning down the phone line. "Have a good day?"

"Yeah, sort of. But I'm much more excited about tomorrow than what happened today."

"What's happening tomorrow?" I asked.

He laughed loudly that time. "I get to see you! Feel you. Take you to bed. God, I've missed you."

I leaned back in the couch cushions, enfolding myself in his warmth. "You sure you don't wanna see me tonight?"

He groaned. "Gah, I'd love to, sweetheart. But I'm going to pull an all-nighter to get everything done so we can have most of the day together tomorrow. I'm sorry."

I sighed. "Sounds like a fair compromise."

"It is. Don't worry. My aim it to have a lot less work long-term, but while you're in college and I'm running off my feet, I may as well make hay while the sun shines, yeah?"

I nodded. "Yeah. True."

Though, my education was still another three years. Did that mean it would be like this the whole time? With me begging for one night with him?

"You okay?" he asked, concern coloring his tone.

I brushed away the feelings of disappointment. I'd been the one to push to come up this weekend. He had plans and yet he'd still accommodated me, so I shouldn't complain.

"Yeah. I'm fine," I said. "Just tired."

"Whose house are you staying at tonight?" he asked. "Or I should really ask where I'm picking you up tomorrow?"

"I'm at my dad's." I said, then suddenly realized the stupidity of that choice. "Is that okay? I can meet you at the beach or somewhere else"

"No. It's fine," he hurried to say. "I'll come up and say hello to Pat. May as well get all the awkwardness out of the way."

I giggled nervously. That would be fun. Not. "Okay. What time?"

"Noonish?"

"Perfect," I said and got up off the couch because I couldn't sit still now, nervous energy pulsing straight through me.

"See you then, beautiful."

"Don't work too hard. Bye."

We hung up and I needed to do something constructive with my energy, so I went and took a shower and washed my hair. But my mind wouldn't stop throwing up scenarios about how tomorrow's meeting between my father and his best friend would go.

How was my dad going to handle Axel coming here to pick me up for a date?

I wasn't sure, but I was going to find out soon enough,

I got out of the shower, into my pajamas and was just sitting down on the couch with a book when Dad came home.

The door opened and he sang out, "Hey, sweetheart! I'm home."

"Hey, Dad!"

He walked down the hallway and into the living space, a bright smile on his face. "How was your night?

"Quiet but good. How was yours?

He put his keys down on the counter and ran a hand through his hair. "Yeah… good."

"Hot date?" I asked as a joke more than anything else.

But then his face went all startled and worried. "Yeah. Sort of."

I frowned. "You look really nervous. What's wrong?"

"Nothing. Just not ready to talk about it, that's all. Too new."

I tilted my head. "I never really understood that expression. Do you mean it's too early to tell if it's going to last?"

"Yeah, pretty much."

I sighed. "I think that's a bit of a cop-out."

"Oh, yeah? You're an expert now?"

I laughed. "Hardly. But I always figured that you can tell within an hour or two with most people whether you're going to be friends or not. And same with romantic relationships. So? Do you like her?"

He nodded, "Yeah, I do. So, I suppose I'm just nervous."

"I get that." My father hadn't been in a serious relationship since my mother. Well, not serious enough for me to have met a girlfriend, anyway. "Dad… did you ever want to get married? Have more kids?"

"Huh?" He bent his head and ran a hand through his hair. "What's with the third degree, Chastity?"

"Sorry!" I rushed to reassure him, jumping up from the couch. "I didn't mean to interrogate you. It's just that since being with Axel, it's made me think more about life and relationships. And you and Mom."

"What about us?" he asked, crossing his arms over his chest in a defensive way.

I slapped my hand into my forehead. "Shit. This conversation isn't going well at all. Let's start again. Dad, how was your day?"

"No," he said, dropping his arms down. "It's okay. Continue the conversation. Why are you worried about your mom and me now?"

I shrugged. "Because I've just realized that I'm almost twenty-two, and neither of my parents even re-married. And I suppose I'm just worried that it's my fault that you missed out on having more kids or getting married. I don't know."

The sadness rose up inside me, then I covered my face with my hands. "I'm sorry."

Dad came over and grabbed my arms, squeezing my biceps. "Hey. Look at me."

I dropped my arms. "What?"

"I never regretted the choice we made to have you, sweetheart. Yes, perhaps I would have gotten married and had other children, maybe… I'll never know. But I love you. Okay?"

I nodded. "Okay, Dad, but don't you ever—"

"No, I don't. I have a great life, and a daughter I'm proud of."

I smiled, though my chin trembled. I didn't like to think of how much my parents had missed out on because of me. Of the choice they'd made in keeping me.

I took a deep, trembling breath, and wiped my eyes. "Okay."

"Good girl," he said, then walked away towards the kitchen. "Let's break out the chocolate stash I kept from Christmas."

I laughed at him. My health-nut father had a chocolate stash. Awesome! "Sounds great."

We ate and chatted about nothing in particular, and when I went to bed, I was happy.

THE NEXT MORNING, I SLEPT IN AND STAGGERED TO BRUNCH AROUND eleven am.

"What are your plans for today?" my father asked over Eggs Benedict at a local diner.

"Well, Axel's coming over soon to pick me up," I said, staring down into my iced hot chocolate, then flicking my gaze up to his frozen face.

"Oh, yeah. That's right. He's taking you out for dinner."

I nodded, sucking the milk through the straw. "Yep."

"And what time's he coming to get you?" Dad asked.

"About noon."

He glanced at his phone. "Shit. That's soon."

"Yeah."

We kept eating, and the conversation stopped.

"We've still got an hour," I said. "And I can tell him to come later, if you want?"

"No. No… it's fine. Where's he meeting you?"

Oh, crap. "He's coming to the apartment to pick me up. He thought he should come say hello."

My dad froze with his eggs halfway to his mouth. I watched as a golden drop of yolk gathered then slid down onto the plate once more.

"Is that okay?" I asked him.

Dad put his fork down and straightened up. "Okay, honey. You need to be straight with me. How serious are you guys?"

"You really want to talk about it?" I asked. Because I wasn't sure my father wanted to know.

His head jerked in a version of a nod. "Yes. I think I have to know, or this isn't going to work."

I put my hands down into my lap and stared at him. I was pretty sure I was going break my dad if I told him the truth, so maybe I should just ease him into it slowly. "We're serious."

He narrowed his eyes at me. "What sort of serious? You guys have only known each other for a couple of weeks."

"Well..." How did I say this without telling him Axel had offered to get me pregnant and look after me financially for the rest of our lives together? "He's taking me to Vegas for my birthday next weekend, and he bought me a car and got an apartment around the corner from school."

Dad put his hand down on the table and began to drum his fingers along the tabletop in a classic nervous tick he had.

"Vegas is cool. You'll have a great time. But none of that is unusual for Axel. He throws his money around to impress girls all the time. Always has."

Ouch!

I glanced down to take a moment to remove the dagger he'd thrown at my heart.

I looked up again. "Dad, can you trust me when I say that we're serious? That we have no intention of breaking up."

"Has Axel told you as much?"

I nodded, inhaling deeply through my nose. I didn't want to tell my father all the things Axel had told me. Partly because they were private, but also because if we broke up in six months because of a fight or we just weren't working out, I didn't want my father to have anything to hold over me.

He sighed. "Okay... I'm going to take your word for it, but I want to tell you one more time that I don't think he's the relationship type, sweetheart. He's just too old to learn new tricks."

I pushed my half-eaten breakfast away, my appetite gone.

"So... what? Why are you telling me that? Again?"

"Because I don't want you to say in six months that I didn't warn you."

He threw some cash down onto the check and I sighed. "Consider myself forewarned Dad."

Standing, he hoisted his jeans up from low on his hips. "Then let's go. You need to introduce me to your boyfriend for the first time ever."

A shot of happiness pierced the sadness and I jumped to my feet. "Brilliant, Dad. Let's go."

Chapter 6

Axel

I WAS RUNNING LATE, WHICH I HATED, BUT IT COULDN'T BE HELPED THIS morning. Fucking business meeting ran an hour overtime, so now I was racing to get ready.

I had a quick shower and threw on some black jeans and a light pink t-shirt. Something young and fun for the day that was significantly different from corporate attire.

I glanced at the clock. Noon. "Shit." I was supposed to be there already.

I shot off a message to Chastity to let her know that I was running late and jumped in the car. My gut was tight with nerves and anger. Patrick hated when I was late for our stuff, so I was gonna cop shit from him too about being late today.

By the time I pulled up outside Pat's house, my gut was a twisted knot.

I got out of the car and pocketed my keys and headed up to the apartment I'd been to a hundred times. But this time it would be for a totally different reason.

I was going to my best friend's place to introduce myself as his daughter's boyfriend.

I shook my head as I jogged up the steps, running a ragged hand through my hair.

"Fucking hell."

This was such a dumb idea.

I entered Patrick's level and walked over to his door, my heart pounding from the exercise and the stress.

I lifted my hand to knock on the door and caught myself hesitating. I shook my head at myself, again, and knocked hard. We'd already been through the worst. Pat had seen me naked with Chastity already. He'd walked in on us, seconds away from actually fucking.

Today would be awkward, but nowhere near as horrifying as that day had been. For all of us.

The door opened and Chastity stood on the other side, beaming smile and golden skin tempting me.

"Hey, beautiful," I greeted, reaching out for her and dragging her into my arms for a kiss.

That first press of her lips on mine had me moaning and sighing into her. God, it had been a rough week. But as I held her and kissed her, everything else floated away—the stress, the exhaustion—leaving only the need to love her.

I pulled back and smiled down at her. "I missed you."

She wrapped her arms around my neck and smiled up at me. "I missed you too."

I glanced towards the kitchen. "Should we go say goodbye to your dad, then head off?"

"Sure," she said, pulling away. "What are we doing this afternoon?"

I lifted my eyebrows up in a suggestive way. "Well, I thought we could get re-acquainted then maybe go to beach?"

"Re-acquainted?" Pat repeated as we stepped into the living room. "You're showing your age there, Axel."

I turned and looked at Chastity's dad, a guy I'd known for over ten years. Whom I'd gotten drunk with, even scored on some chicks together.

And now I was here, presenting myself as his daughter's partner. Weirdest feeling ever.

I tugged Chastity into my side and wrapped my left arm around her. Then I extended my right arm and held out my hand. "Hey, Pat. Happy New Year."

He stared down at my hand and I waited, my heart thudding a little bit too hard.

He reached out and shook my hand, his face solemn. "Nice to meet you."

I grinned. "This is a bit fucked up, huh?"

His face cracked into a smile. "Hell, yeah."

I glanced down at Chastity, then eased my grip on her. "Do you mind if your dad and I have a quick chat?"

She pulled out of my arms, worry clear in her eyes. "Yeah, of course. I didn't have a shower this morning before breakfast, so I might take a quick one now."

She backed away, then turned and fled.

Pat sighed heavily, deflating like a balloon. "Shit, man… my head is completely fucked up." He ran both hands through his hair. "Trying to talk to you like my friend but having to treat you like the guy sleeping with my daughter."

He turned away and went straight to the fridge. "I think I need a drink."

I followed him into the kitchen and pulled out a stool to sit on. "Go for it. It's past noon."

Patrick took down a bottle of whiskey from above the fridge and turned to me. "You want one?"

I shook my head. "Nah, gotta drive." And having sex with a twenty-one-year-old takes concentration.

Pat splashed some whiskey into a tumbler and downed it.

Whoa.

Then he poured himself another.

"Look, man," I said, guilt beginning to ride me. "I promise you… neither of us wanted this."

Patty leveled me with his gaze. "Then why, Axel? Seriously."

I sighed. "Because she makes me happy, man. Like seriously,

nothing else matters when I'm with her happy. And I've never felt that before."

I heard the shower start and looked straight at him. "Look, I'm serious about this relationship. I'm already in talks to sell part of the company so I can back off on the hours I work."

Pat's eyebrows climbed his forehead. "Bullshit. You wouldn't do that."

I shrugged. "Already doing it."

Patrick shook his head. "I never thought I'd see the day you'd settle down."

I huffed out a laugh. "And I'm sure you never thought it would be for your daughter."

His head shot up and he stared straight at me. "No…" he began slowly. "I definitely never thought that."

I licked my dry lips and stood up from the stool. "Can I grab a bottle of water?"

"Yeah. Sure." Pat turned and grabbed one out of the fridge behind him and slid it over the counter. "You have to understand why I'm concerned, Axel. I mean, you don't do relationships. Never have. And Chastity is so young, and she's got so many plans. You've gotta make sure you don't get in the way of any of it."

"I won't," I declared, grabbing the water bottle and taking a swig. "I want to support her in whatever she chooses to do."

"Yeah, but you're rich," Pat said, crossing his arms over his chest.

I groaned. "And I can't even pretend I'm not, can I?"

He chuckled. "Nope. I'd say I know all of your faults and your virtues."

Fucking hell. This was worse than any job interview I'd ever been to. "So, you know I work hard and I haven't committed before. But I love her, Pat, and if she'd let me, I'd just take care of her for the rest of her life."

"But her education—"

"I said, if she'd let me," I said, butting in. "But she won't. She's independent and wants to make it on her own. And I respect that."

"Good!" Pat said, his arms still crossed and defensive.

I sighed. "Look, bud. The only way I'm going to prove to you how serious I am is with time. When I'm still around in three months, three years, thirty years."

"Thirty years?" Patrick grinned, finally lowering his arms. "You really expect to live that long, old man?"

"Hey!" I exclaimed. "You're older than me."

He laughed, and the serious tension in the atmosphere broke. "Okay, Axel. I'm going to give you the benefit of the doubt. But if you break her heart, just know I'll make sure a weight bar falls on you at the gym when you least expect it."

I grinned and nodded. "Deal."

The door to one of the bedrooms opened and Chastity popped out, wearing a flowery long dress with thin straps and a hesitant smile. She looked spectacular. "You two okay out here?"

"Yeah, we're fine, beautiful." I put out a hand and gestured at her to come closer.

She came straight to me, wrapping her arms around my waist and glancing up. "You ready to go then? I packed my bag."

I nodded, smiled at Pat and held out my hand. "Thanks for the talk."

"Likewise."

He shook my hand and showed us out.

I sighed. That had been surprisingly awkward, but better than expected.

When the apartment door shut, Chastity turned to me with her eyes wide and her mouth grinning in a huge, wide smile. "What just happened?"

I shrugged, tugging her towards the stairs. "I think we have an understanding."

I opened the door to the stairs and together we began to jog down the stairwell.

"Yeah, I'm sure you do," Chastity said with a laugh. "He thinks we won't make it through the first month."

I followed her down to the ground floor then grabbed her hand

and led her towards my car, which I'd parked out the front. "You're right. He doesn't."

And I didn't blame him. If I was in his shoes, I'd be worried too.

We jumped in the car, and I turned to her. "So, gorgeous girl, where to?"

She turned her head and stared straight at me, her gaze alight with desire. "To your apartment, and to bed. Please."

I groaned out a growl and started the car. "I was hoping you'd say that. You don't want lunch first?"

"Nope. Home, please."

I raced through the streets and found myself laughing with happiness as we wove around the other cars.

When we got to my parking garage, I zoomed into my spot, jumped out of the car and went to open the door for her, but she'd already gotten out herself, so I grabbed her as soon as she walked around the hood.

"Can't wait till we get upstairs, huh?" Chastity asked, going up on her toes to put her arms around my neck.

"No way," I told her, grabbing hold of her luscious ass with both hands and hauling her against me.

I couldn't wait a minute longer. I dropped my head and kissed her, loving the moan she immediately made as she curled her fingers into my hair and held me tightly to her. I swept my tongue into her mouth, loving the way she wiggled against me, aroused and hot.

I pulled back and grabbed her hand, guiding her towards the elevator doors. "Come on, I want to take you somewhere clean."

We got into the lift and the doors closed, then Chastity turned to me, her cheeks flushed with heat. "There's just something totally hot about the idea of having sex in your car… or on the hood or something. We might get caught!"

I dragged her into my side, glancing up at the security camera in the corner of the elevator. "This place's security is tighter than Fort Knox, so we'd definitely get caught. But if you're set on it, I could order the guys to turn off all the cameras in the parking garage on the day you choose, but I don't want anyone watching us. Or you."

"How come?" she asked as the doors to the penthouse dinged open.

Cupping her gorgeous face, I told her the truth. "Because you're mine. Now let's go inside and I'll show you how much I love you."

Swinging her up into my arms, I walked into the apartment, the door shutting loudly behind us.

Chapter 7

Chastity

Being back with Axel in his apartment, with his lips against mine, was a dream come true, quite literally. When we'd broken up after Christmas, I'd been afraid I'd never see him again, let alone feel his body against mine. But now look at us… I was back!

He carried me into the main bedroom, and I sighed as lust coursed through my body. This was exactly where I wanted to be, and who I wanted to be with.

Axel set me on my feet and cupped my face to kiss me tenderly.

I groaned with frustration, not wanting soft and tender. I wanted him. *Now.*

I grabbed for his shirt and tugged it up, placing my hands against his hot skin beneath.

He moaned against my lips and although he sounded surprised, he didn't stop my hands. I grabbed for his belt, making short work of the buckle, then the button and zipper of his jeans. He pulled back and grinned at me as he tugged his shirt over his head.

Yes! That's what I'm talking about.

I pushed my spaghetti straps down over my shoulders and shimmied until my dress pooled around my ankles. I hadn't worn a bra because I didn't need to, so I stood before him in only my sandals and a pair of black lace panties.

"God, you're beautiful," he said, cupping my breasts with his big, warm hands.

I jumped at him, wrapping my arms around his neck and pressing my naked breasts against his chest. I groaned, loving the feel of him.

He grabbed my ass and lifted me up against him, then walked the few feet to the bed and threw me backwards.

I landed with a bounce and moved up the mattress to lie down. "Panties. Off. Now."

I scrabbled to push the black lace down my thighs and lie back on the bed, completely naked.

He pushed his jeans down his legs and stepped out of his socks and shoes. He stood looking down on me for a minute, his hungry gaze roaming over every part of my body as I wiggled and ached for him.

I didn't close my eyes. Quite the opposite, I stared back at him. He looked even more cut than last time I'd seen him naked. His stomach was washboard flat, with abs that stood out against his skin in defined rectangular slabs.

And that v-thing that ran down either side of his waist, over his hips and beyond. *Damn, that is just so sexy.*

I bit my lip, contemplating running my tongue along that indentation and making him moan for me.

I held my arms out and arched my back, thrusting my breasts into the air. "Come down to me."

He grinned and knelt on the bed, prowling over me like some big, dangerous cat.

When he was right over me, I looked up at him, loving the way he covered me completely. I also admired his strength as he held himself above me, his arms bulging with muscles.

"Please," I begged, reaching up and dragging him down.

When he pressed against me, the heat of his skin made me gasp. "God, I love that."

He grinned then he kissed me, making heat unfurl inside my belly.

Then he moved down, pressing his lips to my neck, my throat, then worked his way down to my nipples, where he stopped and loved on me for too long.

"Please," I begged, tugging at him, needing him inside me, reassuring me that we were back together, and that everything was okay.

"Hang on a minute." He rolled away, going to the side drawer and grabbing a rubber.

He sat up, ripped it open, and expertly rolled it on over his thickness.

I pressed my lips together in frustration, not liking the look of that, or the feel of it. But he was doing the right thing by both of us, so I needed to focus on the why, and it was because I'd asked him to.

When he crawled back over to me, I opened my thighs and welcomed him into my body with a sigh.

"I love you," he whispered into my ear as he nudged my legs further apart and slowly sank into me.

I gasped at the feeling as he thrust all the way in, filling me up and making my belly tighten with pleasure.

"I love you too," I whispered, clinging to his back and wrapping my legs around his hips, wanting him deeper.

He moved faster and harder, stoking the flames of my arousal higher until the only sounds in the room were moans and groans, and the slapping of flesh against one another.

Heat trickled down the backs of my thighs, my core heating and tightening until I couldn't control it any longer. I let go, my orgasm cresting over the mountain of pleasure and for a single moment, everything was quite frozen in time. Then the spell broke, and I was sliding down the other side and into sensation.

I cried out, shuddering in his arms as my pussy contracted around him.

He fucked me harder, making the pleasure last longer and longer, until ripples spread out everywhere, drugging my mind and sating my body.

Then he thrust deeply and froze, groaning over me.

I grabbed his ass cheeks and held him tightly into me, then he collapsed on top of me, panting hard. I stroked his hair and dug my fingers into his back, never wanting him to leave me. But he began to stir, reached between us, then pulled out of me.

It was a strange and shocking feeling. I felt empty now. "Aw, I wanted you to stay."

He chuckled as he rolled over and stood up. "Gotta get rid of this. Give me a minute."

Pulling the condom off his cock, he disappeared into the bathroom for a minute then returned.

I shivered, cold now. So, I slid beneath the covers then threw back the blanket for him. "Coming back?"

"Definitely." He jumped into bed, lay on his back, and pulled me into his arms.

I put my head on his chest, into the crook of his shoulder, and my hand on his heart. He was still breathing hard, and his heart thundered under my palm.

"Bit of a workout, huh?" I asked.

Axel laughed, picking up my hand to kiss my fingers, then placed it back on his pec. "You, woman, are the hottest thing around."

I giggled against him, loving the compliment. "I doubt that but thank you for saying it."

"You okay?" he asked.

I nodded, then tilted my head back to look up at him. "Yeah. I just... I don't like the condom thing. It feels weird, then you leave so quickly afterwards. I think I'll get to the doctor this week and organize some birth control."

"Sounds great," he said with a sigh, wrapping his arms around me. "I prefer having nothing between us, too."

I closed my eyes and let the exhaustion of the session settle over me. Every part of me felt so good. So happy, warm, and relaxed.

"You wanna sleep for a bit?" he asked.

"Yeah." I sighed. "Are you up for a nap too?"

He kissed the top of my head. "Hardly. You've got me buzzing with energy. So how about I tuck you in and come back when you're awake? I don't want to wreck your bliss with me jumping around."

He lifted up and removed his arms from around me.

"Hey—I don't want you to leave." I reached out my hand for him and struggled to open my eyes.

He pulled the blankets up over me and kissed my cheek. "Sweetheart, I'll just be in the living room. You sleep and come out when you're ready. But I want you well rested, because I'll be making love to you all night tonight."

"Oh, okay." That sounded like a plan, I suppose.

I closed my eyes and cuddled into the pillow. A little rest wouldn't be a bad thing. Every part of me felt heavy and totally satisfied. I needed the energy for tonight.

He woke me a few hours later by climbing back into bed with me. He lifted the blanket, which wafted cooler air over my hot skin, and he reached for me.

I crawled closer and cuddled into his bare flesh. "Hmmm… have you come back to sleep too?"

He chuckled and kissed the top of my head. "Well, we have to be at dinner in an hour and a half, and it'll take about thirty minutes to get there, so I figured you might want to wake up soon."

My eyes popped open. "Shit! I totally forgot about the dinner!"

He laughed. "Yeah, I figured. And you know, I could always cancel."

"No," I said, sitting up in bed and yawning loudly. "I brought my new dress that Tony picked for me. And, oh God, I need to wash my hair!"

I threw the covers back and ran for the bathroom. I could hear him laughing from the bedroom as I turned the shower knobs and got the water going.

"I thought you were a girl who could get ready in ten minutes?"

I stuck my head out the doorway and playfully glared at him. "I can! For anything except a fancy dinner. I've got to try a bit harder for tonight, and at least wash the sex off me."

He just grinned at me and crossed his arms behind his head, lying on the bed and not moving. Freaking men! All they had to do was throw on a suit. No makeup or hair straightening for them!

I glanced at the clock. Five-thirty. Shit! I'd slept half the afternoon away.

I ran to the shower, washed my hair and the stickiness from my body, then the race was on. Dry hair then straighten, makeup, clothes, shoes.

I was racing around, and it built up a sweat that messed with my foundation, but I was almost ready before him. I was slipping my feet into my high heels just as he was pulling on his suit coat.

"You look amazing," he said, his appreciative gaze sweeping my body.

I grinned and flipped my hair over my shoulder. "So, what's the deal with tonight? Will it be all business? Social? Will the wives like me?"

He laughed and held out his arm. "It's mostly business, but the women will be there to keep the conversation flowing."

We walked towards the elevator doors. "And the women?"

He snorted. "They're going to hate how young and beautiful you are."

I straightened my shoulders, "I've dealt with women like that my whole life." Namely my mother. "Let's do it."

And we headed down the elevator and into the car, off to my first dinner as Axel's official girlfriend.

Chapter 8

Axel

Walking into the restaurant with Chastity on my arm was an exhilarating moment. She was fucking gorgeous, so everyone looked at us. With her long blonde hair and curves for days, I was hard pressed not to stare.

She also clung to me like she would never leave my side, which also felt fantastic. But when I got to the table and my two colleagues' wives looked at her, I knew we were in for a rough night.

The claws came out as their eyebrows lowered, their gazes narrowing over Chastity like she was a gnat they needed to squash.

Shit. I knew it. Why did I bring her to this thing?

I was considering turning her around when Max stood up and walked around the table to shake my hand.

"Axel. How are you doing?"

"I'm great, Max, Thanks for asking. This is Chastity." I indicated to the gorgeous young woman on my arm, and tried not to wince as the wicked witch of the east rounded the table and glared at my date.

"Axel." Margaret nodded at me, her tone so frosty I would have shivered, except I knew her too well to worry.

I smiled broadly at Max's wife and squeezed Chastity's arm to reassure her. "Margaret, this is Chastity. Sweetheart, this is Max and his wife. Max and I have been in business for—"

"Longer than you've been alive." Margaret snapped, then chuckled softly as though she were joking.

She wasn't.

Chastity didn't miss a beat. "Oh, I doubt that. I know he looks young, but Axel isn't that old." She extended her hand to Max, who was looking at my girlfriend like he wanted to give her a tongue bath. "It's nice to meet you."

Max shook her hand, then I pulled her away to meet the other pair.

"Brian. Nice to see you," I greeted my friend, whose wife was also about twenty years younger than him. The difference was Brian was about seventy now, which made Sharon the oldest of the three women.

"Chastity, this is Brian and his wife, Sharon."

Brian coughed and spluttered, then held out his hand to her.

"Very nice to meet you both," Chastity said, shaking Brian's wrinkled hand, then nodding at the stony face of his wife.

I held in the groan. I was proud of my girl so far, but we had a long way to go to get through tonight.

"Shall we sit down and order?" I asked, indicating to the large, round table dressed with a thick white tablecloth and expensive silver place settings.

"Of course," Brian said, leading his wife back to the table.

I glanced over at Sharon while I sat down next to Chastity. She looked different than last time I'd seen her. Thinner, more aged. Hopefully Brian and she were well. I often worried about Brian's health but was in general too afraid to ask personal questions of the old dragon. He was an incredible financial administrator and I figured he'd tell me when he wanted to slow down.

A waiter came around and placed our napkins in our laps, and Chastity picked up the menu, which was all in French.

She laughed suddenly. "It's not translated. How do we know what we're ordering?"

I grinned and took the menu from her. "We order the five-course banquet and eat whatever they put in front of us."

"Five courses?" Chastity repeated, holding her stomach as though she was going to have trouble putting that away. "That sounds like a lot of food."

I was just about to tell her the courses were tiny, and she'd probably be hungry later, but Margaret got in first.

"You don't have to eat anything that goes against your diet. I know how you young girls are about your weight."

She's in bitch mode tonight.

"Margaret—"

Chastity placed her hand on my arm, signaling for me to stop talking.

I did, at her request, and sat back to watch.

"Is there something about me that offends you?" Chastity asked, narrowing her eyes at the other woman.

"No. Why would you think that?" Margaret asked, crossing her arms over her ample chest.

"Because you're sniping at me like I'm some evil witch that's come to steal your husband or something. And no offense or anything, but I'm happy with Axel."

Margaret dropped her arms and sat up straighter, her eyes flashing fire. "Of course, you're happy with yourself. You've tied down one of the wealthiest men in the city, and you're what? Twenty years old?"

Chastity tilted her head as though examining her rival. "You don't need to jealous. I'm sure you were hot when you were my age too."

"You bet your sweet ass, I was!"

Chastity laughed, turning the tables on the other woman. "Well, thanks for the compliment, but my mom always tells me I need to lose at least ten pounds. I just can't. I'd rather enjoy my food."

And to prove the point, she snatched up a warm, white roll and broke it apart, taking a bite and smiling sweetly.

The air went out of Margaret, and she reached for her glass of red wine. "Tell your mother she doesn't know what she's talking about."

Chastity smiled softly. "Thanks."

I stared at the two other men at the table, who looked equally as perplexed as I felt.

Had Chastity just won that round? I hoped so, though it was hard to tell with women.

The waiter came around and we ordered our usual and more drinks and bread. I had the feeling we might be calling an Uber tonight, because I was getting the distinct feeling I was going to drink too much.

"So, Chastity, are you working? Or are you still in school?" Margaret asked.

Chastity didn't flinch. Deadpan, she said, "Oh, I don't do anything, really. Axel wants me to just stay home and have babies. Oh, and play with his money, of course."

I groaned and tipped my wine down my throat.

None of the others spoke and I was the one to glare at her. "Don't put it like that."

I supposed, technically, I'd asked her to do something similar. But offering to look after her surely shouldn't sound like that.

"She's not serious?" Margaret asked me, staring at me like I was the devil.

Chastity picked up her glass of white wine and dipped her head to cover her smile, but she couldn't stop her laugh and pressed a hand to her mouth when it burst out between her fingers.

The whole table seemed to relax at hearing proof that she was joking, which made me even more defensive.

"To be fair, I offered Chastity a life of luxury. She never has to work or worry about money, or anything. Ever again."

And any woman of my past would have jumped at the offer, but not my girl. She wanted to earn her own way in this world.

Sharon turned to Chastity with a puzzled expression on her face. "And what did you say to that?"

Chastity placed her glass of wine down and grinned at the other woman. "I said thank you, but I've got college, then chiropractic school to finish before I can even contemplate babies. And the money…" She shrugged. "That's a whatever type of thing."

"Whatever?" Brian repeated, his eye twitching like she'd hit a nerve. Hit it square on.

Chastity shrugged. "Yeah. I mean, I can make my own money, right?"

"Not like Axel's money, you can't," Brian reminded her, and I cringed. He didn't need to say that. It wasn't necessary.

She shrugged again. "True."

I wanted to laugh at the beautiful way she just accepted their words, but I didn't like the way everyone was looking at her. Margaret's eyes had shifted to catty once more, and whatever truce had been won initially seemed to be forgotten.

The waiter came and served the first course, then the conversation shifted to work. Business, economics, and the women became silent, as they usually did when the men took over.

Chastity didn't speak much until the very end of the night, when dessert came, and she ate the whole thing in about three moans. "God, that's amazing."

Brian finally turned around to her and asked her about school. She waxed poetic about getting into her chosen field, and I was proud of her, but when we were ready to leave, I could feel the sadness behind her smile.

"You okay?" I whispered as we stood up from the table.

She nodded but didn't respond, which I knew wasn't a good sign.

I paid for the table's dinner as I always did, and the six of us walked out of the restaurant together.

"I wish you the best of luck in the future," Brian said politely, though there was a stiffness to his posture that made him seem uncomfortable.

Chastity smiled back at him. "You, too."

"Yes. Good luck, dear," Margaret said, shrugging into her jacket and sticking her nose in the air. "I assume we won't be seeing you again?"

Chastity gaze narrowed and my stomach tightened. "Why's that?"

"Well, a night like this can hardly be interesting for a woman like you."

"A woman like me?"

Margaret nodded. "Yes. You seem sweet, but you have so much going on in your life I'm sure a business dinner with us was boring for you."

Chastity glared at Margaret. "That's not the reason you don't think you'll see me again. It's because you assume Axel will dump me and he won't bring me to any of these stupidly expensive dinners again. Am I right?"

Margaret didn't answer but she stuck her nose in the air even higher, if that were possible.

Chastity took a step closer to the women. "Listen up, okay? I don't give a shit what you think of me. I don't care if Axel's my father's age. And I bet you don't care if I'm a good person or not, which FYI—I am. I'm sure Axel has never brought a girlfriend to one of these dinners before, so I would have thought you'd give me a little more credit than that. But, no, all you care about is making me feel like crap because you're insecure in your marriages and yourselves."

She took a step back and flicked her gorgeous hair over her shoulder. "You won't see me again, Margaret, don't worry. And it's not because Axel and I will break up, but because I won't encourage Axel to work with your husbands or see you, ever again. So go home and chew on that, you stuck-up bitch."

She grabbed my hand and stared up at me. "Can we go home to bed now? Please?"

I wished so badly that I had a camera right at that moment. Then I would be able to keep forever that picture of Margaret's face, just as she looked at that moment. But I didn't, so I etched it into my memory, nodded at my two business partners and walked Chastity out of the restaurant.

I'd take my beautiful girl home and make this up to her. I'd make love to her all night, and through the day tomorrow.

If she wanted to come with me for these events, I'd have to work out a way that she was treated better. Otherwise, I'd be going to a lot of these nights alone, just like I always had.

And that was fine by me.

Chapter 9

Chastity

Saturday night had been truly enlightening to me. It became seriously obvious to me that I was going to be judged badly by Axel's work colleagues. They wouldn't look at me and see a girl who loved Axel. Or someone who worked hard and had potential for her own life.

No, they'd see blonde hair and youth, no brain and gold-digging tendencies.

So, after Axel whisked me home and we had sex on the floor because I couldn't even make it to the bed before I jumped him, I told him I'd skip the business dinners for a while.

He'd happily agreed, and we'd had a great Sunday together. We slept in, went out for breakfast, then had a long, hot, shower session before I headed back to school mid-afternoon. The traffic was a lot better, but God, I was tired. Driving was exhausting, and I was looking forward to getting an early night.

The other thing that had become crystal clear to me over the weekend was the fact that I'd hated the way Axel used condoms every time we had sex. Him having to pull them out of a drawer or something similar interrupted the flow and didn't feel right at all. Not physically or emotionally for me.

So, after I'd had a great night's sleep, I woke up Monday morning and made an appointment to see the on-site campus doctor. She was great. She explained to me about my birth control options and gave me a script for the pill. I had to wait for my period to come, then I could start taking them and we'd be safe to do whatever we wanted, whenever we wanted. I couldn't wait.

The pill taking process sounded simple enough, and my period was due on Wednesday, so although that meant that my weekend in Vegas with Axel might not be as sex-filled as first expected, at least I'd have better control over my body in future months.

Classes were hectic but enjoyable, and I fell back into a normal routine with studies. Only a few more months and I'd be done, and although I couldn't wait for the rest of my life to begin, there was a certain amount of bittersweet to finishing.

Wednesday came and went, and... nothing.

Thursday.

Friday. And my period still hadn't arrived. I was beginning to worry.

I couldn't be pregnant. Not after... what had it been? Once? Twice without protection. This month.

Last month we'd gotten away with it.

By the time the black town car that Axel had organized for me arrived to take me to the airport, I was a bundle of nerves. Maybe I should have bought a test from the pharmacy along the way so that I knew for sure?

"Calm down. It'll be fine. It'll be fine."

I sat with my hands clenched tightly in my lap almost the whole way. Axel had sent me a message during the day to say we were flying to Vegas for my birthday, just as he'd promised me. I'd hardly gotten any work done after that. I'd washed my hair and packed and spent extra time getting ready, so I looked as pretty as possible for our trip.

But as the car pulled off the highway before we hit the city I called out to my driver, Reggie. "Aren't we going to the airport?"

"Yes, ma'am."

"But this isn't the right way, is it? Unless I'm confused." Which I wasn't. I knew my way around the city.

Reggie smiled and glanced up into the rearview mirror. "We're driving to a private airstrip. I believe you're taking a plane from there."

I shook my head and giggled to myself. Of course, Axel had a private airplane. He was rich. Why did I keep forgetting that?

Probably because you'd still like him if he had no money at all.

I stared out the window as we pulled onto the runway. Happiness bubbled inside me when I saw Axel ahead of us, standing next to the plane like he was casually waiting for a bus or something. Seriously, the man looked just as confident in an elegant French restaurant as he did buck naked walking around his apartment. How did he do it?

"Just a moment, ma'am," Reggie said to me as he opened his car door, so I waited, only to have him hurry around and open my door.

I smiled at him as he offered me his hand and I took it, standing up in the cool breeze that ruffled my dress around my legs. "You didn't need to do that."

"I certainly did," he said, and nodded his head. "I'll get your bag."

Axel walked towards me, looking far too sexy in a pair of grey trousers and a crisp, white, casual shirt. The top buttons were undone, and his sleeves were rolled up. As always, he took my breath away.

"You're spoiling me already," I said as he stepped up and I put my hands on his chest then tilted my head up for his kiss.

His warm hands slid around my waist and pulled me close. "I'm only getting started."

He certainly was. The plane ride was all decadence, with imported chocolates, foot spas and champagne.

When we flew over Vegas, my mouth gaped open. The lights that illuminated hotels and casinos were just as incredible as they looked in the movies.

We landed not far out, and a car was waiting for us to take us straight to a hotel.

Axel held my hand as we drove down the Vegas strip. Tears

blurred my vision at seeing the people, the fashions, the sights. It was all so beautiful. Fantastical, really.

"Hey. Are you okay?" Axel asked, squeezing my hand.

I nodded and wiped my eyes with my free hand. "Yes. It's like a movie. I can't believe I'm here."

He chuckled.

I turned to look at him. "What's so funny?"

"You are," he said with a grin. "I love spoiling you with things like this. Your joy is infectious. Happy Birthday."

The car was still moving but very slowly, so I unbuckled my belt and crawled across the huge backseat and into his arms. "Thank you."

I wrapped my arms around his neck and kissed him, his lips moving on mine with a hunger so strong it made me gasp.

The car slowed down, and the driver said, "We're here, sir. I'll get your luggage and meet you inside."

The driver excused himself and I was left inside the car with Axel for a moment. I pressed my forehead against his and sighed with happiness. "I'm so lucky to have you."

He pulled back and stared down at me. "Funny… that's exactly how I feel about you."

He glanced outside, where a waterfall sparkled in the dim evening light. "Shall we go inside? I want to show you this hotel. It's fantastic. Everything that's great about Vegas is here, all in one hotel."

"Oh, yeah? What's the best part?"

"I'll let you decide," he said, and pushed open the car door.

I squashed the urge to sigh. I didn't want to get out. I wanted to stay inside this little heaven and kiss him until we both couldn't breathe.

"Come on," he urged, then waggled his eyebrows at me. "I'll show you the bedroom first if you like?"

"Okay." I grinned and hopped out of the car, staring up at the glamorous posters hanging above the entrance. "Can we go to a show while we're here?"

"Absolutely. We can drink and play blackjack. See shows and

lounge around the penthouse or pool. It's your weekend. Whatever you want to do."

I grabbed hold of his hand and let him drag me inside. I didn't care that all the girls that walked past us stared at Axel like they wanted to devour him. And I tried not to care about the fact the women were all sexy and obvious, and made me feel grossly inadequate, because he tugged me tightly into his side and barely glanced at them.

He checked us in and whisked me up to the penthouse, where the space was ginormous and so plush it almost seemed surreal.

I picked up a sparkly silver couch cushion and hugged it to my chest. "I can't believe we're really here."

"Why?" he asked, grabbing my arm and twirling me around to face him. "Did you think I'd cancel last minute or something?"

I laughed and ran my hands up his thick, solid arms. "Oh, no. I just… this feels like a dream." I went up on my tip toes and kissed him then pulled back. "Though, how did you get away? I know you usually have meetings and things on the weekends."

He shrugged. "I hired a new manager this week. I'm teaching him the ropes and gave him some of my responsibilities for this weekend. Will see how he did when I get back on Monday."

"Ohh, I'm impressed. I wasn't sure you'd be able to delegate much of your role. I know you built your company from the ground up."

He shrugged. "I have more important things in my life now. It's worth making some sacrifices."

I grinned up at him. "Like what?"

"Like having time for you. I think it's about time I had a life. A real life. And that means cutting back on the eighty-hour, sometimes more, weeks."

I ran my hands down his shirt front, popping the buttons as I went. "That's a great idea. But since we're in Vegas and I am absolutely starving, how about we get dressed and go out for dinner?"

I tugged the shirt tails out of his waist band and ran my hands over his hot skin. "Can I touch you?"

"Only if I can touch you too."

That could get messy. "Shower, then?" Screw my hair. I could dry it again later.

"Definitely."

He turned me around and whacked me on the ass. "The shower's that way. Go."

I squealed as I raced into the main bedroom and began to strip out of my dress. "This place is amazing!"

The master bedroom was bigger than my mom's house. With a king size or bigger bed at one end, and a wall of glass windows showing off an incredible view at the other end of the room.

When I got naked, I had a twinge of conscience. "Axel... ah..." Should I tell him I was late? That there was a small yet distinct possibility that I could be pregnant.

"What, beautiful?" he groaned into my ear as he pressed in behind me, one hand going around my waist and up my ribcage to cup my breast as he bit softly into my neck.

My eyes slid closed as his fingers from the other hand found my clit, pressing into my flesh and arousing me even more.

"Let's get to the shower before we make a mess out here."

I grabbed his hand and pulled him to the shower, letting the heat and steam surround us before I wrapped my hand around his shaft and kissed him.

He groaned against my mouth and gasped as I tugged on him.

"Oh, you want it like that, do you?" he asked.

I nodded. "Yeah, I do. Something different."

He dropped his head and kissed me as he slid his fingers between my legs, torturing me with sweet touches and intimate caresses. We moaned and gasped our way to mutual orgasms, his cock wrapped tightly by my hand, my pussy squeezing his fingers.

And as he held me against his chest, hot water cascading over my back, I knew life after this was never going to be the same again.

Chapter 10

Axel

After our hot shower session where I came so hard I saw stars, I grabbed Chastity and dragged her downstairs to show her the sights that can only be seen in Vegas. The buffet-style never-ending food, the flashing, colored lights and the bells and whistles coming from the casino.

My beautiful girl clung to my arm and squealed happily with every new experience, and I loved every minute of my time by her side. There was no pretense with her. No false sophistication.

Every other woman I'd ever been with had been deliberately disgruntled most of the time. I assumed it was their aim to make me try harder, so they were happier. Although, it could have been because they were constantly hungry, too.

Instead, Chastity ate everything in front of her, and she was lit up from the inside with a happiness I'd rarely seen in my life. She had a huge smile firmly in place on her face at every moment.

A hand caught my eye and I glanced up to see Ralph, one of the pit bosses, gesturing at me with a grin. He was inviting me up to the next floor to play at my normal table.

But I wasn't sure it would be Chastity's scene, so I held up my hand to him and nodded my head, indicating I'd be up soon. Maybe.

Ralph went back to his patrons, and I turned to the woman standing beside me with a water bottle held tightly in her hand.

"Do you want to play cards?" I asked indicating towards the high roller tables. "We've just been invited up."

She frowned as she stared at the elevated tables set into the darkness. "Not really. They look way too serious."

I chuckled to myself more than to her. But when she quirked an eyebrow at me in question, I wondered if she knew what they were. " Do you know what those tables are? Chastity shook her head, "No idea. But I *can* tell you that those ladies over there look like they're having a much better time."

She pointed to a group of women in their sixties, with matching pink satin jackets and squeals of delight as they played the slot machines.

I laughed, enjoying her sense of humor. "Yes. But those ladies are playing with dimes."

I turned and pointed towards the tables where I would play when I came to Vegas, especially if I'd brought a woman who wanted to be impressed by how much money I made. And could lose without blinking an eye.

I shuddered at the thought of my past life. What superficial crap I used to think was normal.

"And those?" Chastity asked, pointing to the tables behind me. "What are they playing with?"

I shrugged. "Millions."

"*Millions?*" she repeated, her mouth dropping open. Then she shrugged. "Now I'm super glad I didn't agree to go up there with you."

"Why not?"

"I can't afford to lose twenty dollars, let alone more. And my dad always says that you shouldn't gamble with more than you're able to lose."

I inhaled sharply, pain kicking me in the gut. "You can't afford to lose twenty dollars?"

Chastity and I didn't talk much about money, and I knew Pat did well enough, but was she really so strapped for cash that she would worry about twenty dollars?

Maybe I should take out some credit cards in her name or set up a bank account for her. I didn't want her worrying about a paltry thing like money since I had more than enough for both of us.

She sighed and rolled her eyes dramatically at me. "It's just a turn of phrase. Jeeze, relax."

A tightness squeezed my chest. "I can afford for you to lose some money here, Chastity. Think of it as part of your birthday present and we can go gamble wherever you want. Slot machines, cards, roulette."

I'd never made such a suggestion to anyone before, but it was liberating.

"Oh, the one with the ball?" Her face lit up.

"Yes."

"Oh, yes, please!" She tucked her hand back into the crook of my arm and we went straight to the roulette table.

Well, there went the rest of the night. She wouldn't bet more than a couple of dollars at a time and pouted when she lost. Which was only superseded by how beautifully she celebrated when she won.

I hardly did anything all night, just sitting back and watching her. She barely drank anything, though she was offered every cocktail under the sun by the waitresses who came past.

When the clock ticked over to midnight, I moved in behind her and wrapped my arms around her waist. "Happy Birthday."

She turned to me and grinned. "Is it Saturday already?"

"Yes. Do you want to stay here? Or should we move the party back to the suite?"

She pressed her ass back into my groin. "Definitely bed." She put her hand up to stifle a yawn. "I'm getting tired, anyway."

"I hope not too tired," I whispered into her ear and heard her giggle. "Grab your winnings and let's go."

Chastity scooped up the few chips she still had and tucked them into her purse. "That was such an awesome night. Thank you so much."

"For forty dollars' worth of chips?" I asked, pulling her away from the flashing lights and sparkly sounds of the casino floor. "I'm not sure that qualifies for the word awesome."

"No, not the money." She shook her head. "For all of it. The whole weekend. The plane flight and the hotel room made me feel spoiled enough. But this," she gestured around us, "is amazing. You wanting me to have a good time. Spoiling me. Even if we went home right now, it would still be the best birthday I ever had."

I swiped our room key to take us up to the penthouse, and as the doors closed on the elevator, I pressed her up against the mirrored wall and kissed her.

Chastity didn't hold back. She kissed me hard, running her hands over my shirt and pressing into my ass, hauling me harder her against her body.

When the doors dinged open, I pulled back and stared down at her flushed face. Her red lips.

"God you're beautiful."

She grabbed my hand and hauled me into the room. "Show me. Please."

My girl didn't want gentle, that was obvious, so I reached over my head and pulled my shirt off. I needed to be naked, and so did she.

She gazed at my chest for a moment, then launched herself at me, kissing me hard.

I picked her up and her legs went around my waist, clinging to me tightly. I held her ass and kissed her, spearing my tongue into her mouth again and again, just as I wanted to do to her body.

I walked us into the bedroom and tossed her down on the bed where she scrabbled back, her chest heaving with excitement.

She gasped as she kicked off her heels. "More. Please."

I groaned as I unbuckled my belt, then unzipped and pushed my trousers off my legs, my skin hot and tingling already. I pushed away my socks and shoes, then once I was naked, I reached for her where she sat on the bed.

She squealed as I grabbed her thighs and pulled her to the edge of the mattress.

I pushed her black dress up her creamy, perfect thighs, and

grabbed the sides of her panties, dragging them down her bare legs and tossing them over my shoulder.

That's better.

I wasn't going to get that dress off easily, so I peeled the straps down her arms and exposed her breasts to my eyes. "Fuck, Chastity. You're sexy."

She got her arms out of the straps and left her dress bunched around her middle. Then she reached up for me, and I crawled onto the bed with her.

I dipped my head to suckle her tight, hard nipples, savoring the flavor of her skin, but it wasn't long before she was groaning and tugging on my hair.

"Please. Now. I can't wait."

Damn. Forgot protection.

"I need to get—" I went to move off her to find a condom, but she tugged me back.

"No. It's fine. The timing… please. It's fine. I need to feel you inside of me."

Yes...

I slid between her thighs, and she wrapped her legs around my waist. Then she pressed her wet pussy against me, and I couldn't help my reaction. I powered into her in one long, strong thrust.

She gasped when I buried myself to the hilt, and I stilled, worried I'd hurt her. "You okay?" I whispered into her ear, pressing her down into the mattress with my weight.

She was so tight, so wet, so hot, it was difficult not to come even now.

She nodded, her nails digging into my back. "Don't stop. Please, don't stop."

Fucking hell.

I didn't. I pulled back and thrust up into her again. She screamed and arched her back, gripping me so tightly it was obvious what she wanted. *More.*

I pushed up on my hands so I could stare down at her lust-drugged eyes, and I rode her hard, like I'd never ridden anyone before.

She moaned and gasped and cried out with every roll of my hips. I fucked her forcefully and fast until she was coming on me, squeezing my cock and forcing my orgasm to the forefront of my tingling body.

But I fought the wave back, wanting this night to be as good for her as possible. She lifted her hips with me, wanting more, so I thrust into her again and again, until she came so hard tears leaked down the sides of her face.

The look of wonder in her eyes was my undoing.

I thrust home one final time and came inside her. Hot, wet, torrents of pleasure pulsed through me, and her pussy squeezed me hard, milking my cock until there was nothing left to do but collapse on top of her and thank God, or whoever had sent me this precious woman.

She was the best gift of my life.

Chastity

After the best sex of my life, I slept like a log then woke early the next morning, nervous butterflies flapping their wings inside my belly. I had to find out if I was pregnant. It was time. For my sanity.

What will Axel say?

I managed to roll away from Axel without waking him, which was always difficult because he clung to me in sleep.

After I got away, I grabbed some casual clothes and raced to the elevator. It took me down to the lobby, where I met one of the many staff members, a blonde woman in her twenties.

"Could you help me please?" I asked her.

"Of course, ma'am. What do you need?"

I dropped my voice to a whisper. "I need a pregnancy test. Do you have any drugstores around here?"

The woman nodded and her fake smile disappeared. "Yes, of course. There's one on the next level down. How about I walk you there?"

"Oh, not if that's too much trouble."

The girl smiled at me, and this time there was a lot more genuine warmth in her face. "Not at all. Happy to help. Come this way."

I followed her down, chose the pink box with three tests because I assumed I'd need more than one, and bought it.

The girl was still waiting for me as I came out of the shop with my brown paper bag.

"Are you okay?" she asked, biting her lip.

I nodded. "Yeah, I am." Terrified, but kind of excited too.

"So, this will be a good thing?" she asked, nodding towards the bag.

I sighed. "Not exactly planned, or on my schedule at the moment, but…"

"The father?"

I smiled. "He will be ecstatic."

The girl, whose name was Daisy if her name tag could be believed, laughed. "That's unusual for the woman to be worried and the man to be the happy one."

"Yeah, well, we're not your average couple. Thank you again for your help."

Daisy nodded at me. "No problem. Good luck!"

She headed off and I went to find an elevator that would take me back to Axel, and the next great decision of my life.

I assumed Axel would be happy, but what about my parents?

What on earth were they going to say when they found out I may have, possibly, made the same mistake they had so many years ago?

Don't get ahead of yourself. I chastised myself. *Gotta do the test first.*

Chapter 11

Chastity

AFTER WALKING AROUND IN CONFUSED CIRCLES FOR TOO LONG, I finally asked someone how to get back to my room. Everywhere looked the same, and I seriously had no idea how to find our elevator again.

But once again, I was found and escorted to my destination by one of the staff.

"Thanks so much," I said to the second blonde girl to help me today, and rode the elevator up to the penthouse.

My stomach was in knots as I gripped the paper bag holding my tests.

The doors dinged open, and I walked into the apartment.

"Hey, birthday girl! Is that you?" Axel called out, strolling into the living area where I now stood, wearing nothing but his birthday suit.

On my birthday. So that was kinda funny.

I found myself giggling at my own joke, and he grinned as he lifted his chin. "Everything okay?"

"Yeah. Of course. But what would you have done if I'd been housekeeping?"

He shrugged. "Tell them I was waiting for you to come back to bed. Then I would have gotten them to send out a search party."

I walked over to him and ran a hand over his warm skin, loving the feel of his huge muscles beneath my palms.

"Are you coming back to bed?" he asked, reaching out to grab my waist and hauling me against his naked body. "Or did you go searching for food because you worked up such an appetite last night?"

My stomach wavered with nerves. "Ah… I've gotta go to the toilet actually."

I hadn't gone this morning because I'd been so anxious to get out the door as soon as possible. Now, I was busting.

Axel stepped back and stopped squeezing me. "Oh. Sure. Then what? Bed first? Or breakfast buffet or both?"

My brown paper parcel was held tight in my hot little hand, and I knew it was time to reveal all.

With my heart in my throat, I ripped the paper off, opened the box and took one of the long sticks out. "Should I assume this is pretty self-explanatory? Or do you think I should read the instructions?"

Axel's jaw dropped.

Anxiety pulsed through me. My chest squeezed tightly, and my bladder ached to go to the bathroom. Not a great combination.

"Is that what I think it is?" he asked.

I pressed my lips together. "Hmmm. Well, depends on what you think it is."

"Are you pregnant?" he asked, taking a step towards me, the joy in his face hard to miss. His eyes were sparkling, and his mouth turned up in a grin.

"I don't know yet," I said, taking a few steps towards the bathroom. "I have to go pee first."

"Then go pee!" he practically yelled, with a happy grin on his face.

I ran, laughing with hysteria the whole way to the bedroom ensuite.

I shut the door to the bathroom and raced over to the toilet. Ripping off the foil wrapping, I stared at the strange piece of white plastic. "Definitely should have read the instructions."

It was too late now though. My bladder had decided it was time to go, and urgency overtook my movements.

I pulled the cap off the end, sat down and peed on the stick like they said to do in the movies.

It was strange and not exactly clean, but in the end, I had a wet pregnancy test, and my bladder was empty.

"Thank God for that."

I put the plastic cap tip back on and set it down on the vanity to wash my hands at the sink.

"Anything yet?" Axel called out from the other side of the door.

I shook my head. He was too much. "You can come in, you know."

The door swung open, and Axel stood in the doorway, wearing his jeans this time.

I raised an eyebrow at him. "Thought you should get at least partially dressed, did you?"

"With news like this I was debating making a cocktail."

My heart fell and I glanced down, unable to meet his eyes. "That bad, huh?"

"Hey, hey… I was joking." He crossed the huge bathroom to cup my face. "I love you. I want to spend forever with you. A baby would be—"

"Unwanted? Too early? Totally unplanned?" I threw at him, just the first few words my brain came up with.

He stared straight into my eyes. "It would be amazing."

He bent his head to kiss me, and I lifted my chin, needing the contact. The reassurance.

I reached for him, grabbing onto his waistband, wishing I could strip him of the jeans and climb on top of him right there. But before I could do anything of the sort, he pulled back again and tilted his head as he looked at me. "You know, if you really don't want this, we don't have to do it. It's your body, Chastity, and your choice."

A lump rose in my throat as my eyes burned with tears. "No, I couldn't."

Get rid of my baby? Axel's baby? I just couldn't. Not for the sake of going to chiropractic school. Not for my parents. No.

He pulled right back this time and grabbed my hands tightly. "Moment of truth then?"

I nodded. "Yep. I'll grab it. I hope I can decipher the results. Maybe I should have brought the box in with me."

"I'll go get it," Axel said, and turned to leave the bathroom.

I picked up the piece of plastic, a strangely excited feeling hitting my stomach as a hysterical laugh bubbled up. "I don't think I need the box."

It wasn't one line, or two, a cross or a plus sign. Nothing vague or hard to decipher with this one.

Axel turned back. "How come?"

I handed it to him. "Because it spells it out for you."

Axel lifted the pregnancy test and stared at it. I knew what he could see. The same thing I had. One word.

PREGNANT.

His gaze flicked up to me, and he was un-naturally still as he asked. "You're pregnant?"

My hand went unconsciously to my flat stomach and pressed hard. "Ah…"

"You're pregnant!"

Hot tears rose into my eyes then fell down my cheeks, a wave of unexpected emotion crashing into me. I sobbed as he hugged me tightly, and I let more tears fall.

"It's okay. It's going to be okay," he said, cuddling me tightly, and laughing softly. "I hope this doesn't mean you're as devastated by this news as you sound?"

I pulled back and shook my head. "No." I gulped and turned away to grab for the tissues in the box by the sink. "I'm just… I don't know. It's a lot."

Blowing my nose, I then took some deep breaths to calm myself. I'd been feeling overly emotional this week. Now I knew why.

I splashed some water on my face and patted my cheeks dry with a nearby towel. "Are you happy about the result?"

I had to ask him, even though I knew the answer. Suddenly there was intense need to surround myself in positivity. It felt like I was going to need him to get through this choice in one piece.

"Me?" he repeated. "I'm very happy. To have a baby with your heart and soul, your eyes… that's the dream, Chastity. But if this is the wrong timing for you. If you'd rather wait until you've finished your degree, it's your choice. I won't be the one to push you to keep it if you don't want to."

"Oh, I do want to!" I rushed to reassure him.

He was extra sweet to offer me the out, but it wasn't an option for me. Not now.

"You do?" The hope and love in his eyes were almost heartbreaking. I'd never thought anyone would love me this much.

I nodded. "Of course, I want this baby. It's your baby. But… all my plans. My parents."

I shook my head sadly as the tears gathered again, making my heart ache.

"Come on. Let's go sit down." He took my hand and walked me out of the bathroom and back towards the bed.

We sat down facing each other, and there was a comfortable silence that stretched around us like a soft cloud.

"You know," I began, wanting to change the topic for a moment. "I love being with you. Even just like this, holding hands in the quiet. It's really nice. I've never been this comfortable or happy with anyone before."

And there was so much more to it. I wanted only good things for him. Happiness, health. And I wanted to be there for him. And not for the parties, and the fun, and the glamor. I wanted to be there through all the dark moments.

If this was love, then let me have it forever.

"I feel the same way as you," he said, suddenly serious. "Honestly, Chastity, whatever you want, we'll do it."

I swallowed the tightness in my throat. "This isn't just about me. What do you want Axel?"

"What do I want?" he repeated, like he was surprised I'd asked.

I nodded.

He sighed. "I want to work week on, week off, so I can enjoy you and not miss out on so much. I want to travel. I want to buy you the perfect family home where we can let our kids run. Not some high-rise apartment without a tree in sight."

"Really?" I asked, a lump in my throat making me swallow awkwardly.

"Really."

There was a long silence.

"So," he began, "are we heading down to breakfast? Your birthday is only just beginning. I have lots of ways to spoil you today."

I nodded, feeling the tightness in my chest ease for a moment, and my hand finding its way naturally back to the flatness of my belly. "Okay, let's do my birthday. Then we can talk about this more later."

He stood up and held out his hand. "Definitely. I have a feeling it's all we'll want to talk about for a long time to come."

I got to my feet, a sick feeling in my stomach. "I know. It's hard to think about anything else."

Like how the hell I was going to tell my mom. My dad... my professors. Shit. They were all going to be so disappointed in me.

He smiled and I melted a little. "That's because it's exciting. And amazing. And going to change our lives in the best way."

I took a wavering breath, trying to will some courage into my heart. "You're really excited by this?" I quirked an eyebrow at him. "When are your lawyers gonna come running at me with a pre-nup?"

He grinned at me as he reached for a blue shirt and pulled it on. "That's for a marriage."

"Oh." Now I was embarrassed. "I didn't mean it like that. I just meant aren't people going to worry that I did this to get your money or something?"

I didn't know what I was saying. But I did know I was going to get a lot of flack from everyone I knew. My family, my friends. There would be no way to go on to chiropractic school now.

"I don't give a flying fuck what anyone else thinks," he said, and there was a conviction in his tone I envied. "All I care about is what you think, and what we choose together. But as we said, let's leave that conversation for later today. We've got a breakfast to devour. Then a show later tonight."

"Give me one sec." I quickly changed into a light summer dress and sighed. This was the start of a new chapter for me and for Axel, and I honestly had no idea how it was going to end.

Chapter 12

Axel

Taking my newly pregnant girlfriend to breakfast was an entirely new experience. I watched her like a hawk, a million questions rolling around in my mind. Was she supposed to eat fried bacon? And wasn't there a rule about cheeses that she was to avoid now? I had no idea and felt stupid opening my mouth to ask her. She probably wouldn't know either. Surely, she wasn't far enough along to worry about those things yet? We needed to get her in to a specialist as soon as possible. I was sure one of my friends would know a good obstetrician.

We sat down in one of the many restaurants this hotel boasted. I watched her take a sip of water and a memory of last night's casino fun tugged at me.

"Hey, sweetheart. Did you know you were pregnant last night? Is that why you barely drank anything?"

Chastity put her glass down and shrugged. "Yes, kind of. I had my suspicions, but I didn't actually *know* yet."

"But that's why you weren't drinking?" I asked to clarify. I loved the fact that she was protecting our baby already, even though to her last night, it had only been an idea. A possibility.

She nodded. "Yeah, I know it's bad for the baby, and the last thing I wanted to do was take a risk."

"Even though you didn't know if you were going to keep it?"

She nodded and a small smile quivered on her lips. "Let's be honest here. I was always going to keep it. The idea of losing that connection to you when I love you so much is, well… I can't even fathom it."

"Then tell me what's still worrying you." Because it was obvious by her slightly somber mood that something was playing on her mind this morning. Her smiles weren't the usual wattage.

A waiter walked up to our table, and we turned to give him our attention, ordering food and hot drinks off the menu, then turning back to one another.

"Go on," I urged her. "Tell me what's bothering you."

She glanced down at the table and ran her fingers over the silver spoon in front of her. "I think it's just the whole pregnant at twenty-one thing. Well, twenty-two, anyway. But I haven't even finished college yet. Just like my mom," she said, her voice cracking as she said "mom," then she picked up her glass to take another sip of water.

Her eyes were looking suspiciously shiny and I wondered how much had been said to her over the years about her parents' "mistake" in getting pregnant so young.

I had to tread carefully here, because this was it. The crux of the issue. I could see that Chastity had other hurdles to overcome, and her education was one of them. But this admission that she was going to be seen the same way her mother had been—young, and stupid—was the real problem.

I thanked the waiter as he delivered my coffee and Chastity's hot chocolate, and picked my mug up.

"I think our situation is quite different, sweetheart."

Chastity rolled her eyes, then took a sip of the hot chocolate, a milk moustache imprinting on her top lip for a moment before she licked it clean.

My gut tightened with desire. The things that woman had done with her tongue had been utterly amazing. And I couldn't wait to get her back into bed so I could love her more.

"Yeah, we are different. But my parents had been together for almost three years before they had me. We've been together a month!"

I chuckled. "So? What's the timeline got to do with it? Your parents obviously weren't meant to be together, or they still would be."

A nagging voice at the back of my head said that I should say something to Chastity about Pat hinting he was getting back together with his ex. After twenty years apart, it seemed ridiculous that they would want to be together now, but what did I know?

Chastity picked up her knife and fork and began cutting up the buttermilk pancakes and syrup that she'd ordered. "Timing means a lot, actually. Everyone will know that we didn't plan this, they'll call you stupid and me slutty, and it'll be a whole ridiculous thing."

She forked a piece of pancake and ate the bite, her moans of delight making me smile.

"Good?"

"Oh, yeah."

I sipped my coffee and watched her eat, loving the way she dug into the food. "Sweetheart, look. Like with everything in my life, I'm not going to give anyone the time of day who disagrees with how I run my life. I stopped giving a shit about other people's opinions a long time ago."

She raised an eyebrow, and in between bites, asked, "So, you're not going to care that your friends and probably your family are going to think that I'm trying to trap you? That I got pregnant on purpose?"

I grinned at her. "God, no. I'm going to tell them all that I was the one who got YOU pregnant on purpose and I had to hurry, before you ruined my plans to trap you and went on the pill."

Her hand froze mid-air, her mouth hanging open. "Seriously?"

"Yep. I'd much rather them think I wanted to trap you, than the other way around." Which wasn't too far from the truth in regard to the fact that I wanted Chastity however I could get her. For the first time in my life, I felt lucky to have a woman. This woman. And I wasn't letting her go.

She took a bit of pancake, chewing thoughtfully, then said, "Is that true?"

"That I *planned* to impregnate you?" I laughed at the thought. "Of course not. I've heard from various friends that have gone through years of IVF that it can actually be difficult to get pregnant. But we did have unprotected sex multiple times and I admit that I didn't mind the idea of having a baby with you right from the start. And now that we are? I'm elated."

She picked up her glass of water and sighed. "You know, I feel really sorry for those couples who have to spend tens of thousands of dollars to have one baby."

"Try hundreds of thousands," I corrected her, finally picking up my cutlery to eat.

Her eyes bugged open. "Are you serious?"

"Very," I said, cutting into my eggs. "I know at least three couple that have spent six figures to get one child."

Chastity's hand slipped down to her belly. "So, we've already saved a hundred thousand dollars by getting pregnant naturally?"

I laughed. "That's one way to look at it, yes. And as far as the timing like goes, sweetheart, I don't want to wait five years to be with you and hold our child just because society thinks you should date for years before committing to someone. I knew the moment I saw you that you were the woman I wanted in my bed, then when you spoke with that quick wit and smiled at me…" I shivered. "I was done for."

She laughed and pushed her plate away, sighing again. "I really hope my parents aren't disappointed in me."

I stifled the groan that rose. "Sweetheart, there is absolutely nothing for them to be disappointed in. You've found a man who loves you, can easily financially support you and our child, and who desperately wants this baby. What else is there?"

She wrapped her hands around her mug of hot chocolate once more and pressed her lips together. She wasn't convinced.

I sat up straighter in the high-backed chair. "Look, how long before you have to tell people? I'm sure we can wait a few months. Just until you are feeling secure, and safe enough to share."

Surely by then she'd want to tell everyone.

Chastity met my gaze and I could finally see a sparkle of happiness there. "You're right. I have months to decide how to tell people, and I'm sure I can still finish my college degree while pregnant. I'm not due until… hang on a second."

She grabbed her cell phone and began tapping away.

I waited, having no idea what she was actually doing.

"Ah, October fourth. Approximately. Oh, yeah, that's a lot of time."

October fourth sounded like a perfect day to me.

She was looking happier now, and I wanted to take advantage of that and make sure she stayed that way. "Perfect. Now, I have a lot planned for you today. I've booked you in for a facial and a massage with the hotel's spa, and we have tickets for tonight's show."

"Really?" she asked. "You've gone all out for my birthday!"

I grinned at her. "That's only the beginning. I want to take you shopping for a real present, of course, and get you a ring to go with that necklace of yours." I waggled my eyebrows at her, then dropped my gaze to the single diamond nestled above her cleavage.

"You want to buy me a ring?"

I nodded. "Yes, I do." I'd propose marriage right here and now if I thought she'd say yes, but she was reacting like a deer in the head-lights during every new conversation, and I didn't want to scare her off. She already thought I was crazy because I wanted this baby so much. "But just as a birthday present. Maybe we can call it a promise ring?"

"A promise ring?" she repeated, her fingers going to clutch the floating diamond at her throat.

I nodded. "Yes, it was all the rage in my parents' era. A promise ring was the first sign of commitment. Then the engagement ring, wedding ring, and eternity ring, of course."

I watched her throat work as she swallowed hard. "And you… are thinking about all of those steps?"

"Of course, I am," I said, reaching across the table and squeezing her hand with mine. "You're the woman I want to spend the rest of my life with, and you're carrying what I hope is the first of our children."

Her eyes were all shadows and doubts, so instead of forging on with the awkward proposal, I just smiled. "But one step at a time, yeah? A tradition must be kept. So first, a promise ring. My only question is, would you like me to choose something that goes with your necklace and present it to you at dinner? Or would you prefer to go shopping with me and choose something yourself?"

Her eyes lit up this time as she smiled at me. "That's such a thoughtful question."

I shrugged. "What can I say? You bring out the best in me."

Which was such a stark contrast to any of my exes, who'd definitely brought out the worst.

"Why are you asking though?" she questioned, grinning cheekily at me. "Afraid you'll choose wrong?"

I barked out a laugh. "No. But this is something I want you to wear every day, so you have to love it. It only makes sense to ask you to choose it. Although… if you'd rather a surprise."

"No! I'd actually love to come shopping with you."

"Done," I said, glancing at the time on my cell phone. "We probably have enough time to hit the slot machines before your pamper package and I'll arrange a viewing at a jeweler for the afternoon."

I'd need to go to Tiffany's. They didn't advertise their prices, which I knew would affect her choices. I didn't want her choosing a piece based on the price, and knowing her, she'd pick one of the cheapest rings they had.

I wanted her to love it. Price wasn't a factor, or a limiter.

"Axel, thank you."

"You're welcome, birthday girl," I said with a grin, then pushed my plate away. "Where to first? The slot machines or roulette again?"

"Actually," she said, "I'd love a quick shower before the day spa. Wanna join me?"

Abso-fucking-lutely.

She stood up with a sultry smile and I grabbed for her hand. We had an hour.

Oh, all the things I could do to her perfect body in an hour.

Chapter 13

Chastity

I'D NEVER BEEN SO PAMPERED IN ALL MY LIFE. I HAD A LUXURIOUS FACIAL with an older woman named Trixie, then a massage with another woman called Celine.

The day spa was quiet and serene, with music playing gently in every room and water flowing over rocks in the foyer. It was nothing like being in Vegas in the movies, and yet it was only here that I felt totally relaxed about being waited on hand and foot. At home I would never have been able to justify such luxury.

"You're all done, so take your time getting up and I'll see you out front," Celine whispered in the quiet of the room, squeezing my shoulders one final time.

"Thank you so much," I told her, barely able to open my eyes.

That massage had been incredible, and I was so sleepy and relaxed I didn't want to move.

But Axel would be waiting for me, and he'd said he was taking me shopping. What an idea, Me, choosing a diamond ring for my birthday present. It was just an insane idea.

It felt like I was living some sort of fairy tale at the moment, because this wasn't my life. It couldn't be.

I forced myself off the table and got dressed again, a lethargy that was bone-deep making my arms drag as I pulled on my clothes.

My hand strayed once again to my stomach, and I pressed my palm firmly against my flesh. My tiny, tiny baby was inside me growing, safe and sound. But what if something bad happened? What if I lost it? How would I feel then? Relief? No.

My stomach plummeted and I had to swallow hard to stop the bile that rose. Miscarriage was common, wasn't it?

I needed to look it up. I didn't want to lose this baby. Even if the timing meant that school was going to need to be postponed and all my friends and family would think I was nuts. I wanted this, with Axel. We would be a family and for me, there was nothing more important.

I grabbed my cell phone and headed for the door of the massage room. I stepped out into the foyer and grinned as Axel walked towards me. His hair was damp, and he'd changed clothes.

"Hey, gorgeous. How was your massage?" he asked, reaching for me.

"Amazing." I loved the way he stepped up and slid his arm around me in that possessive habit he had.

I reached for his face, which was clean shaven and still slightly damp. "Did you have a shower again?"

"Yeah. I went to the gym for an hour and needed another."

I smirked at him. "Only you would feel the need to train on vacation."

He leaned forward and whispered in my ear, "Gotta keep fit for you."

I slapped at his chest playfully. "Hardly."

He pulled back and grinned. "Shopping time? Or are you ready for lunch?"

I was a little hungry, but I could definitely wait. "Shopping, please."

He slid his hand around my waist and pressed his palm to the base of my spine. "This way."

He led me out of the day spa and into the brightness of the casino levels once more. We wove through the assortment of people, and I found myself grinning like a loon.

There was a happiness bubbling inside of me that made me a little ashamed. I loved my cheap clothes and costume jewelry, but there was something ridiculously exciting about being spoiled by the man I loved. And the intent of where he was taking me, shopping to buy me a ring, was just the best.

A promise ring, he'd called it. A universal sign of commitment. Something I could wear and rely on, which said to anyone who dared question us that he loved me. And he wanted us to be together for a very long time.

"In here, sweetheart," he said as we reached one of the most well-known and expensive jewelers of all time.

"Oh, no," I said, slamming on the brakes and stopping us in the middle of the walkway. "They'll be way too expensive."

He slid his fingers from my waist once more and gripped my hand instead. "No, it's not. And how about we make a deal that until you're my wife, you let me worry about how much money I spend, and how?"

"Your w-wife?" I repeated, suddenly feeling more anxious than excited.

My mother would *kill* me if I married someone after knowing him for two months. Was that why we were in Vegas? Oh God!

He laughed loudly, a sparkle twinkling in his eye. "Don't worry, I won't ask until I'm sure the answer will be yes. So how about you just let me worry about my money, and I'll let you worry about yours."

"Okay." It probably wasn't fair to tell him how he could spend his money, but surely there were cheaper options. "But—"

"If you won't come and pick which one you want, I'll just choose myself," he said with a sigh and what looked like a reluctant shrug.

I narrowed my gaze at him. "You're baiting me."

He put a hand to his chest. "Me? Why, I'd never."

I glared at him this time. *Smart ass.* "Fine. Let's go."

It was my turn this time to drag him into the shop, and I was blinded by the brilliance of the lighting. "Whoa." I put my hand up to shield my eyes, part of me wishing I was back in the tranquil setting of the day spa.

"Can I help you, sir?" a woman in front of us asked, and Axel slid up to the counter and spoke softly to her.

I raced forward to try and catch the last of their conversation, but she was already moving around the shop and opening all the cabinetry.

"What did you say to her?" I asked as I watched the woman look in and under every glass box.

"That we were looking for a birthday present."

I waited but he didn't say anything else, although I was pretty sure he'd said a hell of a lot more to the woman, but what hope did I have of finding out?

And why was I fighting this anyway? Axel had more money than he knew what to do with. He'd already bought me a diamond necklace, a car and an apartment. Surely, a simple little ring could be added to the list of his gifts.

"I've taken out a selection of our newest, most modern rings. Were you interested in only white diamonds, or perhaps you wanted something with color?"

"Color?" I repeated, stepping closer to the display she was arranging before me.

Wow.

"Yes, we have canary diamonds, pink diamonds, and of course, this three-stone ring that has two brilliant cut sapphires on each side." She picked up a ring and held it out to me.

It was white gold or platinum and had three large stones across the top. One diamond, with a blue sapphire on each side.

"Um…" I reached out for it and held it in my fingertips.

"Do you want to try it on?" Axel asked.

I wasn't sure. I didn't like blue or classic rings like this as much as the intricately designed, ornate pieces.

"I would prefer something less classic."

I set the ring down and peered at the display of massive stones in front of me.

"These are beautiful, really. But they all look like engagement rings, and I was hoping for something more simple."

Axel and the saleswoman exchanged a look, then she flurried off once more.

I turned to him. "What was that about?"

"Nothing."

"It wasn't nothing. What did you tell her?"

He sighed heavily, obviously not wanting to tell me the truth. "I told her that you deserved the best and that money was no object."

He looked crestfallen, and guilt hit me hard in the chest. There was nothing worse than someone throwing your gift in your face.

I slid towards him, wrapping my arms around his waist and staring up at him with all the adoration I was feeling for him hopefully clear in my eyes. "I love you for this. How about I make you a deal this time? I won't think about the money if you don't either. I'll choose something I love, we go with that one, no matter what. If it has a hundred diamonds on it or none at all."

"Deal. But you've gotta try on at least ten different rings. That's my only rule."

"Done!"

The saleswoman hurried back with a grin on her face. "I have scoured the store for our most unusual rings, and I hope you don't mind, sir, but I also found a few pieces in our antique collection."

I almost groaned. Of course, she did. And they were probably the most expensive rings in the store.

I threw my hands up, noticing straight away that absolutely nothing had a price tag attached to it.

Like my mom always said, *"If you have to ask how much it costs, you can't afford it."*

"I'm very adverse to him spending this sort of money," I explained to the saleswoman, "but I have been overruled, so let's do this."

I tried on more than ten rings, probably closer to thirty. Rings with flat bands, and intricate designs. Rings with massive stones, and ones with pink, yellow and white diamonds.

In the end, I chose a ring I wouldn't have thought would be the one. It was rose gold with two vines of leaves on either side. It had white diamonds and pink sapphires and sat so beautifully on my finger that I didn't want to take it off.

"I, um, think this is the one," I said, through a throat clogged with emotion. I kept extending my arm out to stare at it and felt a strange type of intense emotion sweeping through me every time I looked at it.

"Do you want to put it in the box?" the woman asked, offering me a classic Tiffany-blue square shaped ring box.

I pulled my hand back and curled my fingers into a tight ball to stop her from taking it away from me. "No, I'll wear it."

Axel chuckled and picked up my hand, pressing a kiss to my fingers. "It's perfect. Happy Birthday."

Tears filled my eyes as I went up on my toes to kiss his lips. "Thank you."

Axel went with the woman to pay for my gift, and I wandered to the other end of the store because I didn't want to know how much it cost.

I wanted to focus on the intent behind the gift and the love I had for my family that was growing by the day.

We had a whole day ahead of us, and most of tomorrow too.

And I for one was going to enjoy every minute of this, and maybe consider it our first babymoon!

Chapter 14

Axel

The rest of the weekend went by too quickly. We ate rich food that had me aching to return to the gym. We gambled some money away and went to a show.

Chastity was perfect company the entire time. During the day she was fun, and cute, and stuck to my side like glue. During the night, she made love to me with a single-minded focus that made me want to tuck her into my body and never let her go.

But according to her, she *had* to return to school, and that stuck in my craw something fierce.

"Are you sure you need to go back?" I asked her once more as we descended the stairs off the plane at the private air strip I owned.

I took her hand and glanced over at the two cars in front of us. I had to get back to the city, and my car waited for me.

She was determined to return to college, and her driver waited for her by the black town car. She bit her lip and ran her hands up and down my arms, not answering.

I gave it another shot. "You know, you don't actually have to finish the last six months, sweetheart. I can buy you a business or whatever you'd like to manage. You don't need a degree to work with me. I'll teach you everything I know."

And that was something I'd never offered anyone before.

She frowned up at me this time. "And what? Tell our baby that I'm officially a college drop-out, and that I never finished because I got pregnant? I don't think so."

I inhaled sharply at her tone. I wasn't going to win that argument. It was obvious she wasn't really talking about us, but from her own personal experience growing up.

"I understand but I'll miss you," I said, touching my forehead to hers and drinking in the last of her warmth.

"It's only five months," she reassured me. "Not even, really. Then I'll be finished, and we can focus on us and our family."

I smiled as she stepped away and went to pick up her bag.

"You'll have a nice bump by then, I hope," I said, letting my gaze linger around her still tiny waist.

Her hand came up and pressed against her belly button. "You're right! Thank goodness those graduation gowns are roomy, yeah?"

I nodded, a lump coming to my throat. She would look so beautiful heavily pregnant with her large belly and swollen breasts. I couldn't wait until I had her next to me in bed with all her womanly curves on display once more.

"I love you," I told her, unable to stop myself. She grinned and launched herself at me once more.

She kissed me hard, and I gave back twice as much, pressing her lips apart and tasting her tongue, wanting to get as close to her as I possibly could.

But too soon she was pulling away. "I love you too," she whispered. "And hopefully I'll see you next weekend. Maybe down at the apartment near school if you can drag yourself away from work?"

"I'd love to," I said, though I had a sinking suspicion I'd have a lot of work to do this week to make up for the weekend I'd just taken off.

Hopefully now, because you only live once, and I was pretty sure moments like this were few and far between in life.

In fact, I knew it to be true.

"Drive safely," I called out, then looked away.

Damn I was turning into a soft cock. What the hell?

She got in the car and the driver drove away, and I stomped over to my sports car and jumped in. She'd turned me into some mushy, half-wit. And it needed to stop.

Now.

Sure, I'd miss her this week, but she had studying to do, and I had a company to run. Surely, that would keep me busy enough not to worry about her too much.

I turned on the ignition and got on the phone to make some calls.

I'd hired a new manager this week, and I was hoping he'd done at least half the work I'd assigned him.

If he had, I'd at least be able to sleep tonight. If he hadn't, well, I wouldn't.

As my shit luck would have it, he'd done a lot less than half the work I'd assigned. In fact, he'd royally fucked up two deals, and had knocked off at noon on Saturday and taken the rest of the weekend off because to quote the pompous dickhead, "I deserve days off to rest."

Not when I trusted him with my company he didn't. So, I fired him on the spot, then went home and got to work.

I worked all night, making multiple international calls and video chats trying to right the wrongs my ex-manager had accomplished in my absence.

I got about twenty minutes sleep around six am, then kept going through the rest of the day.

It was disheartening to say the least. Not the fact that things had gone so wrong. That happened all the time in business. I'd learned to roll with the punches, take the hits when necessary, and knowing the long game was the only game worth playing.

The true problem lay in the fact that I now knew for certain that I couldn't trust anyone to do my job. I simply couldn't step away from my business the way I wanted to. It was too risky unless I took the time to groom someone to be me, but that would take months. Years, even. If it were even at all possible. Without a stake in the business, there was no driving force that would compel anyone else to work the way that I did.

But it wasn't just me anymore. I couldn't just run my life from dawn to dusk and back again, around my business. I had Chastity now, and the baby. How was I going to be a company CEO, a partner, and a father? And all of them well?

I didn't think Chastity would appreciate the little amount of time I would have for her once she was through college and lived with me full time, which I assumed was the plan though we hadn't talked about it yet.

But that was a puzzle for another day, because I had no answers tonight.

Monday night came, and although my eyes felt like they were being held up by matchsticks, I reached for my cell phone and called my woman.

"Hey! I was just thinking about you."

I instantly smiled and for a moment, my exhaustion seemed further away. "All good things, I hope."

"Oh, yeah. Definitely," she said, a smile evident in her voice. "How was your day?"

"Ah… good, overall."

"You sound tired," she said just as I was closing my eyes and running a hand through my hair.

I laughed. "Yeah, I am."

"You should sleep. I'm sure you stayed up all night working. Can you get an early night?"

The question hung in the air. Could I?

"I've got a lot of work to do."

"But you could probably do it tomorrow." she urged, interpreting my tone and words correctly.

I shook my head. "How do you read me so well?"

She laughed. "I don't know. Maybe because I care about you."

"Just care?" I asked, teasing her for her word choice. I hoped she did a hell of a lot more than just care about me. I was besotted with her and was hoping the feelings were returned.

I stood up and stretched my back, then walked over to the kitchen to make a quick protein shake. Once I got some food into me, I could probably go to bed. She was right.

She sighed softly. "I don't mean I don't love you, because I do. But I mean, I actually care if you're well and healthy. If you're happy or working yourself into the ground. To me, that's more."

I smiled as I shook the protein shaker and headed to my bedroom to strip off.

"I don't think anyone—and I'm counting my parents in this as well —I don't think anyone has actually cared about me before."

"Seriously?" she asked. "Well, then I'm not looking forward to meeting them. What horrible people."

I grinned. "Yeah, well, they'll want to meet their grandchild for a minute, then they'll be off traveling the world again, so don't worry. You won't have to put up with them for long."

"Hmm… I'm not sure if I should be happy about that, or sad."

I shrugged. "It is what it is." I'd come to terms with how shit my parents were years ago.

I kicked off my shoes and sat on the bed.

"Are you getting ready to go to sleep?" she asked.

"Yeah, I'm just getting ready now." I tugged off my shirt then lay down on the bed. "How are you feeling today, sweetheart?"

"Oh, I'm good. No nausea or anything yet, but I made another appointment with the doctor to tell her why I can't go on the pill anymore."

I grinned. "Yep. That ship has sailed."

And for me, happily so.

"Hey," I began, closing my eyes because they were too heavy to hold open any longer. "After graduation, will you move in here with me? Or we can buy something else if you want. A house with a back yard maybe?"

We'd need to move further out of the city and away from my building, but what was an extra ten-minute drive?

"Are you asking me to move in with you?" she questioned, her voice breathy and light.

"Of course, I am," I told her, though my enthusiasm was probably lacking in my voice due to exhaustion. "I'd have you move in this week if you could. But I know you need to graduate first."

"I'd love to move in with you in May," she said. "And I adore your apartment, but I'd much prefer a house if we could get one."

I snorted. If we could?

"Anything you want, sweetheart. It's yours. Just look at what's for sale online, and as long as it's not too far away from my work, it's yours."

She inhaled sharply. "Easy as that?"

"Yep," I said, feeling a wave of tiredness washing over me. "I want you and the baby to be happy." And if she wanted suburbia, with its large backyards and flowerpots, then we'd get that.

Though, I didn't want her running herself into the ground either, so maybe it was finally time to hire a housekeeper.

I yawned loudly. "I'm sorry, sweetheart, but the sandman has come. I'm not going to be able to stay awake much longer." In fact, I could feel my brain spiraling into the darkness even as I said the words.

She chuckled softly. "I love you. Talk to you tomorrow?"

"Definitely."

I didn't remember hanging up the phone, but I must have at some point, because the next time I woke up it was almost ten hours later, and Chastity's sweet voice was still ringing in my mind.

Chapter 15

Chastity

I STARED AT THE DOCTOR IN DISBELIEF. "DID YOU JUST OFFER ME A chemical abortion?"

The woman before me blinked at my tone. "It is my obligation as your doctor to give you all the options available to you. Going ahead with the pregnancy is not the only one."

I stood up and grabbed my backpack. "I came here for help, not for... whatever this is. I'll see a private doctor from now on."

Who the hell did she think she was? Just because she was working in a college setting didn't give her any right to try to alter my choice.

I turned towards the door and reached for the handle. What sort of backwards thinking was this?

"Those are expensive if you don't have insurance, and I really think..."

I whirled around and glared at her. "The baby's father is a billionaire. Yes, you heard right. A *billionaire*! So, don't tell me I don't have access to the right care. You know nothing about my situation."

The doctor's eyes widened, and she blinked quickly. "Oh, I'm sorry. Your file indicated that you were on a financial scholarship."

I slammed both hands onto my hips and glared at the woman. "I'm on a scholarship because I worked my ASS OFF in High School and got the grades to qualify for one!"

The fact that my parents didn't have the thousands of dollars to pay full tuition was none of her business.

I growled in frustration and stormed out of the office, grabbing my bag tightly to me and leaving the medical building.

I couldn't believe she'd said such a thing! I hurried to my dorm and ran down the hall. Hot tears filled my eyes, and I didn't stop running until I reached my room.

I threw myself on my bed and cried until I felt sick. What a horrible woman! Was this seriously how I was going to be treated by everyone who knew my news? It wasn't like I was extremely young and single. I was twenty-two and had the love and support of a man who loved me.

What else did I freaking need?

I sat up and dashed the tears from my face, anger surging through me now. How dare that doctor—or anyone—assume I couldn't look after my baby. My parents had done it without the financial support of anyone, and they'd done a good job. I tapped on my phone and called Axel, swallowing hard to try to disguise the sound of the tears I knew he'd still be able to hear in my voice.

"Hey, sweetheart, I'm just two seconds away from stepping into a meeting. Can I call you back?"

I inhaled sharply, tears still blurring my vision. "Yes. But I need you to answer one question first."

"What's happened? What's wrong?"

"You want this baby, right?" I managed to ask, dashing away the tears on my cheeks.

"Yes! Absolutely."

"And you'll help me get a good doctor and buy a crib and diapers?"

"Hang on, I'm just telling the guys I need a minute." He put the phone on mute because I heard nothing for a minute, then came straight back to me. "Sweetheart, what happened?"

I shook my head. "Nothing."

"This isn't nothing. Did you tell your mom?"

"Oh, God no." I shuddered. That was going to be a conversation and a half. "I just spoke to the doctor here and she gave me my options."

There was a heavy beat of silence. "Uh... I'm not sure I'm following."

I wanted to roll my eyes, but while I was frustrated, I was impressed that he'd admitted he didn't know what I was talking about.

"The doctor told me how to have a chemical abortion and was of the opinion that was the best course of action."

"They fucking... *what?*"

His anger paralleled mine, and I instantly felt bad for the doctor. She was gonna get it.

"So, I just wanted to make sure you've got my back with the doctors and the hospital and all that stuff."

"Sweetheart, I'll—" He coughed and took a breath. "I'm sorry. Give me a second."

I waited, because it was reassuring to hear that he was as mad as me.

"Okay. I think I can speak now."

I grinned on the other end of the line, my heart light and happy. This was why it was a good idea to be with Axel. Not for his money, but for his heart. His sense of humor, and the sex. Who could forget how good the sex was?

"Chastity, your health is everything to me. So, number one, I will call my insurance guy today and purchase you the top level of coverage. Number two, I will transfer one of my properties into your name, today. You can choose whichever one you want. That will be a financial surety for you, no matter what happens. And, number three, I will have that doctor gone from campus by the end of the day."

"Oh." My stomach dropped. "You don't have to—"

"I do. And it will be done. Give me a couple of hours, and I'll get my assistant to send you a list of properties you can choose from."

"Axel, my love. Calm down. I don't need a property. I just needed your support, and you've given that. Thank you. I feel better." And that was the truth. I could breathe now.

"Oh, I haven't even begun to show my support, sweetheart. I need to go, but you'll receive a message soon from Cheryl. Okay? You met her the other day when you came to the office."

"The dragon at the front desk?" I asked.

He chuckled. "Yeah, that's her."

"Great! I liked her."

He laughed. "You would. Okay. Talk later. Love you."

He hung up and I sat on the bed in shock. Now, that was a man! When presented with a problem, not only did he solve it, he tied everything up in a pretty bow and gave a bonus set of steak knives too.

I got off the bed and reached for the box of tissues to blow my nose. If this was how emotional and unstable I felt this early in my pregnancy, I could only imagine how bad I'd be later on.

My phone rang and I picked it up, not recognizing the number but it was a local area code.

"Hello? Chastity speaking."

"Chastity! It's Cheryl here, Axel's office manager."

"Oh, hi, Cheryl. Axel said you would call but I wasn't expecting you right away."

"Are you busy? Should I call back later?"

I dropped back on the bed with a sigh. "No. Not busy at all. Go for it."

"Mr. Patterson asked me to call you with a list of his properties without mortgages attached. Unfortunately, that list is the shortest one, but there are still a few to choose from."

I sighed heavily and ached to talk to someone with a maternal view on things. "I really don't want one of his properties, Cheryl. He's being over-protective."

"It's not any of my business."

I rubbed my fingers into my forehead, hoping to relieve some of the tension from my head. "Cheryl, I need someone to talk to and get advice from, and as I've told you before, my mom isn't exactly an Axel fan, so could you help me?"

There was beat of silence, then, "What do you need?"

"Okay, my problem is this… Axel wants me to choose a property of his to transfer over into my name, but he doesn't get it. I don't want his money."

"Then why is he doing this?"

My stomach twisted. "How much can I trust you, Cheryl?"

She laughed softly on the other end of the line. "I've worked for Mr. Patterson for almost fifteen years, Chastity. I'll take his secrets to the grave."

Perfect.

"I'm pregnant."

Silence.

"Hello?"

"Ah, yes. I'm here. That's a first."

I huffed out a laugh. "Well, I'm glad to hear that. But Axel's trying to compensate for our lack of time together, and he wants to reassure me that he's not going anywhere and that the baby and I will be taken care of. Which believe me, I appreciate, but I never want him or anyone else to think I'm with him for his money. And I don't need a house or a business. Or anything else like that. So, what should I do?"

"Well, I'll preface my thoughts with the knowledge that you really don't have a lot of say in whether you get this asset transferred over to you or not. Mr. Patterson will do what he likes. But that being said, I don't see a negative in choosing something that could be an asset for you or your child in the future. If you two break up in a year, legally you will be entitled to a settlement and an annuity that will set you both up forever."

I sighed. "Again, not what I want."

"But, if you two are still together in twenty years' time, then that property can be transferred to your baby's name, which will be a nice nest egg. The question of why you're together only comes about if you break up, and if that isn't your intention then you should have no qualms about doing this, because you know you'll never have to cash in on it anyway."

And the penny dropped, so to speak. "You're right, Cheryl. If we're together forever, it's not going to matter."

"No. It won't."

I sighed. Okay. So once again I had to accept this ridiculously expensive gift and hope I never needed it.

"Cheryl, you've convinced me to relax a bit, thank you. So, of the places on the list, which do you recommend?"

"The most expensive one, of course."

I laughed. "No, really."

"Hmmm… Well, for myself, I'd choose the apartment in New York, but if you really want something that will be for pure asset value, then I'd go with the small apartment block in Phoenix. It has great returns and was recently renovated."

"But won't I have to deal with leases and people, and all that?"

"Yes. Would you prefer something here in town? Perhaps for one of your parents to live in, or—"

"Oh, my mother would die!" I shook my head, but then again, it would be a great way to pay her back for everything she'd sacrificed for me. "What did you have in mind?"

In the end I chose a large house near the beach that was currently on long-term lease. I hoped never to need to use it, and instead invite my mom in to live in it when she'd come to terms with me and Axel being together.

But like most people, I had no idea what the future held, so I thanked Cheryl for her help and lay back on the bed, my head whirling.

I was still falling down the rabbit hole and was dizzy from all the spinning.

Chapter 16

Axel

When I'd learned that Chastity had chosen one of the least valuable houses I owned, it didn't surprise me. In fact, I laughed out loud when I heard the result. But at least she'd chosen one, and somehow had gotten Cheryl on her side. I wasn't sure how she charmed people the way she did, but I was convinced Chastity was part witch.

She was magic to me.

I made a few phone calls, got the paperwork moving on the house and called the school to make a formal complaint. Happily for me, and not so happily for the doctor Chastity had seen this morning, I knew several members on the board at her school. They assured me that a different physician would be in place within the week.

I called a friend whose wife had twins and got the name of their obstetric specialist. Chastity would have the best care money could buy. I hadn't worked this hard and this long for nothing. This was when my money mattered. Not expensive homes and weekends away, though those were nice. It was being able to give those I loved the life they wanted, and for Chastity, at least for the moment, all she was concerned about was caring for her pregnancy.

And I adored that about her.

When I got in my car to drive home, I put my cell on speaker and called to tell her everything that had happened during the afternoon. I wanted her to know how proud I was that she'd chosen a house so close to the beach and good schools, so that if she wanted to live there long-term, it would be perfect for us.

But she didn't pick up, so I left a long voicemail and ended up driving home, eating dinner and getting more work done. Why she wasn't answering her cell, I didn't know, and a knot twisted in my gut worrying about her. Maybe she'd been in an accident? Or maybe she'd just fallen asleep early? Pregnant women did that, right?

I was considering calling her mom to see if she'd had any contact with Chastity tonight, when there was a knock at the door. Glancing at the time, I saw it was ten pm. A bit late for anyone to drop by on a Monday night.

I walked over to the door and opened it, happiness flashing through me when I saw who stood on the other side of the door.

"Hey, Pat."

"Hey," he said, looking nervous and not attempting to walk inside like he normally would.

"Didn't use your key this time?" I joked, raising an eyebrow in question.

He huffed. "Never using it again."

I laughed because really, what other choice was there, then held open the door to my friend. "I was just catching up on some work. You want to come in?"

"Yeah, if that's okay."

"Of course." I stepped back to allow him to enter, something I hadn't needed to do for a very long time

The guy who was my best friend, or had been for a decade before I fell in love with his daughter, walked in the door.

"You want a drink?" I asked, pretty sure he needed one if the look on his face was anything to go by.

"Only if you're joining me."

How could I say no to that request? If Patrick was here to talk, I might need the fortification. "I suppose I could stop work for a while. It's been a rough day."

"Oh, yeah? How come?"

We walked together towards the kitchen where I grabbed a couple of beers out of the fridge for us and cracked their tops. "I hired a new manager thinking he could take a load off me so I could get a bit more of a work/life balance, and all he did was fuck up some meetings and make things more difficult. Not exactly what I'd been looking for."

"You're doing… what?" Pat asked, his eyes goggling. "Work/life balance? Who are you and what have you done with my friend?"

I laughed as I handed him the drink. "Yeah, well. I'm getting old."

I gestured for him to follow, and we wandered over to the couch and sat.

I groaned as I relaxed into the cushions. "Shit… it's nice to sit down." I'd been going all day.

Patty grinned at me. "You *are* getting old."

I took a swig of beer and shrugged. "It's time to slow down. I don't want to keep working at the pace I have been. It'll kill me eventually." Of course, before Chastity I'd been quite happy to work myself into an early grave.

Live hard, die young. All that crap.

Patrick leaned forward and rested his elbows on his knees as he cradled his beer with both hands. "What's the real reason, Axel?"

His tone was slow and careful as he asked the question.

I sighed and took another sip of the beer, not sure I wanted to go down that path. "You sure you want me to say it?"

Pat nodded. "Yeah. Gotta hear it, I'm afraid."

He glanced up and met my eyes, and he was deadly serious.

This time I sighed even heavier. My best friend didn't want to know how much I cared about his daughter, he really didn't. But then again, shouldn't a father know how treasured his only child was?

I shook myself and prepared to tell the truth.

"It's Chastity. She's the difference," I said, though my stomach felt like I'd just been punched. I pushed on, "She deserves a good life, and I don't mean an easy life with money and diamonds everywhere. That's not what she wants."

One side of Pat's mouth tilted up. "But I'm sure you've showered her in both. Kaiti told me you took Chastity to Vegas for her birthday."

"Yeah, I did." I swallowed hard, busting to tell my best friend the news I was going to be a father. But it was both too soon in the pregnancy, and not my secret to tell. "I bought her a diamond ring, got the most expensive suite in the place. But I think her favorite part of the trip was spending a total of eighteen dollars over six hours in the casino. Seriously, you should have seen her."

I shook my head. She'd been adorable.

"Sorry. You bought her a what?" My friend was staring at me like I'd grown a second head.

"Oh, it's not what you think," I said once I'd cottoned on to what he was flabbergasted about. "When I propose it'll be with your full consent first. Don't worry."

I wasn't going to make that mistake.

Patrick sat bolt upright. "*When* you propose? Are you fucking kidding me, Axel?"

I swallowed hard and faced off against the man who obviously still didn't think I was good enough for his daughter. "Yeah, I said when. What's wrong with that?"

"But you're—"

"What? Forty-one? A hardened bachelor? A workaholic?"

"Yes!" he exploded. "All of the above!"

I slid to the edge of my chair, anger biting into my jaw. "So what? What's that got to do with the fact that I love her? And I'll make her happy! And just so we're on the same page, I'd propose tomorrow if she'd say yes. But she won't because she wants to finish college first and I fucking love that about her." I shook my head, biting the inside of my cheek. "She's so fierce. And smart. And loyal." I glared at my best friend, her dad. "I love her, okay? More than you obviously realize."

Pat's mouth dropped open, but no words came out. Then he tilted his beer back and drank most of it in a couple of long swallows.

He put the empty bottle down on the coffee table in front of him and wiped his mouth with the back of his hand. "Wow. I mean, I know you've said you love her and all that, but I thought you meant as a passing fancy. Someone to enjoy for a while, then you'd both move on. But you're talking—"

"Forever. Yeah, I am." And it was obvious that Pat needed to hear the truth, because he was living in Lala land if he thought I was playing around.

I crossed my arms over my chest and glared at him. Sure, I'd been out with a lot of women over the years, but I'd never bought any of them apartments or rings, or anything overly personal. God, most of them I couldn't even stand to sleep beside for a few hours.

"Is that why you came over here?" I demanded. "To learn my intentions? Because I was pretty sure I'd made it clear how I felt about her last time we spoke."

"Well, yeah. I mean, it's obvious from what Kaiti said that you two are getting along, but I didn't think you actually saw a long-term future together."

I sat up and glared at my friend. "Why not?"

"Because, well… you're you, Axel. There's no way you'll find the time she needs around your work. And yeah, she's at college for another four months, but what's going to happen when she moves away to study chiropractic? Surely, you're not going to do the long-distance thing. That never works."

I swallowed hard and picked up my beer to take a drink, mostly to give myself time to think about what I was about to say next. I didn't want to lie to my friend but announcing that Chastity wouldn't be able to attend chiropractic school wouldn't go down well either.

"Look, Pat, I want to make it work. I've been looking for the right woman for twenty years, so if it comes down to it, I'll sell the company, move to wherever she is. None of this bullshit matters." I gestured to the expensive apartment around me. "If I don't have her."

Patrick stared at me, his dark eyes full of intense emotion. "She really means that much to you?"

"Yeah, she does. She means everything."

He inhaled deeply and stood up. "Then I think I got what I needed."

I stood too.

He extended his hand to me. "Okay. Then I'll back off and for what's it worth, you have my blessing."

I extended my hand and shook his. "Thank you."

We walked towards the door and as he went to leave, I called out, "So, how are we going to do this?"

"What this?" he called back.

"Us. Are we friends still? Or are you officially my girlfriend's dad, and nothing more?"

Patrick inhaled deeply, then sighed. "I'd like to go back to being friends. I miss training with you. My fitness level has dropped the past few weeks."

I laughed. "I'd like that. So, what? We just talk football and work and shit?"

"Avoid personal talk? Sounds like a plan to me."

I laughed as I shut the door, then sighed. He was so going to kill me when he found out about the baby.

I shrugged. Oh well, he'd punched me before. I'd wear his anger again if I needed to, because I wouldn't change a thing.

Chapter 17

Chastity

I'D ONLY MEANT TO PUT MY HEAD DOWN ON THE PILLOW AFTER MY LAST class for a moment, just to shut my eyes for a second. Then I'd woken up the next morning feeling like utter crap. My head hurt, my body ached, and my stomach squeezed tightly with hunger. I'd missed dinner. Damn it.

"Oh, God." I groaned as I rolled over and reached for my phone. No one said I'd feel exhausted from doing nothing.

I really needed to download some pregnancy apps or get some books. I knew next to nothing about what was happening to me.

I stared at the screen on my phone.

"Oh, Axel." Gah. He'd called multiple times and messaged as well. Poor thing thought something was wrong, which would be the normal assumption to make if I hadn't answered my phone for twelve hours. But in this case, I was okay. Sort of.

Except that your baby is draining the life out of me!

I sent a quick text to assure him I was still alive, then rolled out of bed to stagger to the bathroom. I wasn't sure if he'd get my message right away or not but sent it anyway, just in case. It was still early, not even six am, and technically he should be asleep. Maybe but not likely.

I went to the bathroom, then crawled back into bed. No nausea or anything I'd expect from typical morning sickness, but I just felt sick. Like I had a flu or something. Even my sinuses felt clogged.

You okay? Can I call? Axel messaged straight away.

I sighed. I couldn't do it. Not yet. Plus, Hope was fast asleep across the other side of the room. She wouldn't appreciate being woken up while I tried to talk to my boyfriend.

I managed to text him. **Can I call later? Feeling like crap and need a little more sleep. Love you. xox**

Then I passed out again.

I woke up much later and had to bolt to get to my classes. I hated being tardy and having the lecturer glare at me as I tried to sneak in. But I got through the morning's lessons sipping on water, and anxious to get something to eat.

I went straight to the cafeteria to grab sandwiches and some fruit, then I called Axel.

"Hey, sorry about stressing you out last night," I told him, biting into a crunchy apple. "I meant to just have a nap before dinner, then call you after. I didn't think I'd end up sleeping straight through."

He chuckled. "It's fine, as long as you're okay."

"I'm okay," I reassured him. "Though I'm not sure what to expect next. Maybe I need to see that doctor sooner rather than later."

"I got the name of a great specialist, and my insurance broker has found you an individual plan. You just need to contact him and give him some information, and it's done. If I send you the numbers, can you make an appointment with the doctor and deal with my insurance guy? Shouldn't take too long."

"Of course," I said, grinning from ear to ear. He really was looking after me. "Send it over."

"Great. I have to go, but we'll chat tonight, yeah?"

I nodded even though he couldn't see me. "Thanks, Axel."

"Anytime, sweetheart. Love you."

"I love you too! Thank you! Bye."

I called the specialist immediately and answered the questions the best I could. The receptionist seemed nice enough, though lacking the warmth I was expecting from people dealing in pregnancy and babies.

I texted Axel soon after to tell him that we had an appointment within the next two weeks. Then I set about downloading all the apps and books to get myself up to date on what was happening with me, what would happen in the next few months and years.

All that information was overwhelming in lots of ways, but some apps were hilarious, and I focused on those.

And that was how the rest of my week went, teading and studying for exams. Napping when I needed to and flicking through a dozen pregnancy apps to work out which ones I liked best.

When the weekend came, Axel had to work.

"I'm so sorry, sweetheart, but there's no way I can take another weekend off. Do you want to come here and relax at my place?"

Relax after a two-hour drive and not spend any time with him? Probably not.

"To be honest, I'd be happy to just chill here. I'm behind on my own work because of all the tiredness, and if that's gonna continue through the semester—" And all the books pointed to the fact that tiredness was a major side effect of pregnancy. "—then I should probably try to keep on top of things too."

"Oh, yeah that makes sense," Axel said, though I could hear the disappointment in his voice.

I sighed. "I miss you too. Don't worry. But it's only like... four and a half months until I graduate now." I'd worked it out almost to the day. "Then we can spend as much time together as possible."

Hopefully, assuming he had learned by then to step back and work less.

"That's true." His sigh mirrored my own.

"Hey, have you hired anyone new to help you run your business?"

He chuckled. "Hardly worth it at this point. I've spent the whole week trying to undo the damage the last one caused. I'm not sure I'm cut out to let someone else be me."

I laughed at that. Of course, he thought that way. "Well, they can't be you, that's impossible. But all leaders delegate. And I'd hoped that you wanted to find someone soon, because I'm going to need you when the baby comes."

My mom would pitch in to help, I was sure. When the time came to tell her, and she'd got over the shock of becoming a grandma, that is. But I didn't want Axel being one of those dads who just popped in for five minutes to say hello, then worked the rest of the time.

That wasn't what I wanted for me or my baby.

"I'll be there," he said firmly.

"How?" I asked, sitting up in bed and crossing my legs.

"I haven't figured that out yet."

I rolled my eyes. It wasn't going to work itself out. "Have you talked to my dad? He might know someone that would fit."

Axel sighed. "He popped by last night, actually. I told him I wanted to scale back, and he laughed in my face."

I giggled. "Yeah, I could imagine that. He thinks you're married to your work."

"Well, I have been for a long time. But things are different now."

Horror struck me and I squeaked. "You didn't tell him, did you?"

"No. I thought that you'd want to do it together or by yourself. Either way, it's your call."

Relief swamped me. "Thank you for that. I'm reading all this stuff on the baby and the pregnancy, and it's scary. So many women miscarry, especially their first. I think I want to wait until we're sure everything's okay before we tell anyone."

From what I'd read, some people waited until twelve weeks, some longer.

"Even your mom?" Axel asked.

"Especially my mom," I said, twirling my finger around the pink blanket scrunched up on the bed beneath me. "She's gonna be freaked out enough as it is. But I don't think I could deal with all her emotions as well if I lost it."

The very idea had me tearing up.

"We can do this however you want, sweetheart," Axel said, his voice deep and sexy, yet reassuring at the same time. "Can you send me all the details for the doctor appointment, and I'll make sure I'm there."

"Yes, I'll text you now."

I put him on loudspeaker and tapped in the details. As soon as I was done, Hope walked in the door, so I took him off speaker to put him to my ear again.

"Thanks again for organizing someone. I feel a lot better now."

"No problem. Well, I better get some work done, but I'll call you tomorrow, okay?"

I nodded and stood up, reaching for the covers on my bed. "Sure. I think I'll get an early night again. Love you."

"I love you."

And we hung up.

I reached for my pajamas and began to get changed. My nipples were sensitive, and I was getting teary again, which was bloody annoying.

"Hey, you okay?" Hope called out suddenly.

I glanced up at her, blinking rapidly to dispel the tears. "Yeah, fine. Why?" I still hadn't forgiven her for her juvenile, rude comments about Axel.

"You just look really pale, and you're sleeping all the time at the moment."

I shrugged. "Just run down, I think. It's been a tough couple of weeks, and this last semester is gonna be rough."

She nodded. "Yeah. Okay."

I didn't want her to be the first person to find out about my pregnancy, though if I started throwing up every day, it was going be hard to hide it.

I walked over to our bathroom and closed the door. Time to wash my face, brush my teeth, and go to bed. I glanced at the scale. It wasn't mine, it was Hope's. I'd never been one to worry about my weight. If I fit in my clothes and felt healthy and full of energy, all was well.

But the pregnancy apps said I could gain between twenty and fifty pounds. Did I even want to see that happen on the scale?

I shook my head and brushed my teeth, focusing on the only thing I could control at the moment, and that was what I was going to do next.

Sleep. Eat. Study. That was my weekend.

When I walked back into the bedroom and climbed into bed, I found Hope still hovering around.

"Are you going to bed already?" she asked.

I gestured at my pajamas as though it should be obvious. "Yeah, why?"

"Oh, it's just that there's a party out on the quad, and I thought you might want to come."

I rolled onto my side and faced her. "Look, Hope, I have a boyfriend, and it's serious. So, I don't think I'll be going to any mixers this term."

"Why not? It's just being social."

I groaned and hauled myself up to sitting. "I just wanna get through this last semester, okay? Balancing study and Axel is going to be hard enough." Not to mention the physical demands of a pregnancy. "I just don't need any other pressures, okay?"

"Okay." Hope scurried to the door, then glanced back. "I know you're kind of pissed at me still, so I'm sorry for what I said. I didn't realize you guys were serious."

I sighed as I resettled into bed, my body aching with exhaustion. "I don't think that's much of an excuse, but okay. Thanks for the apology."

Hope opened the door, but still hung around. "Can we go back to how things were? I don't want to fight."

And neither did I. I didn't have the strength. "Okay. But I don't want you making any cracks about Axel's money or his age, or anything like that."

Hope pretended to zip up her mouth.

"Okay, cool," I said, waving at her. "See you in the morning."

"Night." She slipped out and closed the door behind her.

I sighed heavily, my body already relaxing into sleep. Why did everyone give us so much grief on being together? We weren't hurting anyone, and it was nobody else's business.

It shouldn't be this difficult all the time.

Chapter 18

Chastity

The weekend was uneventful, as was the next week. I studied, attended classes and talked to Axel every day. He was busy, but so was I, so I tried not to think about how absent he might be in the future.

I read in one of my pregnancy books that women became mothers when they became pregnant. Men became fathers when the baby was born.

I took that to mean because I felt pregnant, exhausted, and slightly queasy most of the time, the bond with my little one had already begun. For a man, until he could hold his child in his arms and look upon its face, it kind of made sense that the bond wouldn't be the same.

A large part of me was hoping that Axel would check in a lot earlier than after the birth, but hey, I was getting way ahead of myself. I was only six weeks along.

The day of the specialist appointment arrived. I let my professors know I had a medical appointment so wouldn't be in class, and Axel sent a car to pick me up to drive me down to the city. Initially, I'd said I'd drive my car, of course. It made sense.

But when Axel had insisted and I'd woken up that day feeling truly sick, I was grateful for his protectiveness.

I sat in the car with a bottle of water in one hand and a dry cracker to chew on in the other. Why did something so wonderful like growing another human being have to be so torturous on the body. It didn't make sense.

I sighed and put my head back on the head rest, drifting in and out of sleep while we drove into the city.

As we pulled up in front of a huge, white building, I woke up.

The driver cleared his throat. "We're here."

I glanced out the window. "Is this a hospital?"

"Yes. Mr. Patterson will be here shortly."

I pulled out my phone and there was a text from Axel.

Running 5 mins. behind but will meet you in the office. Dr. Martinez. Second Floor.

I sighed. "He sent me all the details. I think I'll go in."

"All right, ma'am. I'll park around the corner and be back to pick you up and drive you home." He got out of the car and came around to open my door.

I picked up my bag and got out

The driver handed me his card. "My cell number, so you can call me when you're done."

I grinned at him. "Thanks."

"Good luck," he said, then walked back to the driver's seat.

I sighed and stared up at the huge white building. I wasn't sure this was the sort of place I wanted to come every month. It looked super impersonal and clinical. But I shouldn't judge a book by the cover, so to speak. Even though literally, everyone did. Otherwise, why bother with pretty cover art?

"I'll see you in a bit. Hopefully won't be more than an hour."

I took a deep breath and trudged inside. I had no idea what to expect. A scan? Blood tests? Or just a chat about what was coming?

I walked inside, found the stairs and walked up to the level that the supposedly legendary Dr. Martinez practiced on.

The office wasn't difficult to find, so when I pushed open the door, I walked up to the reception desk.

"Chastity Lennox for a twelve o'clock appointment."

The receptionist looked through her huge, dark-rimmed reading glasses at me, then towards the computer. "Oh, yes, the new patient. Dr. Martinez doesn't usually accept new patients. You must have a connection to our current patient list."

She pushed an iPad across the desk at me and I took it. "Just fill in the forms and I'll upload them for the doctor."

I didn't have my normal level of energy or sunshine but tried a smile on her. "My partner got me the appointment, so I'll make sure to thank him. Thanks for your help."

The woman nodded at me, but I didn't see much defrosting of the outer layer of crust.

I made my way over to the chairs and sat down, then filled in the forms the best I could. They wanted to know everything from my last period to my insurance, to my weight and goals for the pregnancy.

When the door to the office opened and Axel stepped in, the whole room seemed to turn to look at him.

He stood tall and gorgeous, with an expensive suit and his hair all slicked back. He spoke to the woman at the front desk, who practically melted when Axel spoke.

I grinned as she pointed at me, looking surprised as hell.

Ha! Yep, he's mine.

I waved and smiled at him as he hurried over. "Sorry I'm late, sweetheart."

"All good," I told him as he bent down to kiss me on the lips. "I haven't been called in yet."

"Chastity," was suddenly called into the room by a nurse holding a door open.

I grinned up at him. "Saved by the bell."

I stood up next to him and took his hand, tucking the iPad under my arm. "That's me."

The person I assumed was the doctor, who was a woman in her forties smiled at me and I had an instant sense of relief. "Come this way."

"I'll just take that from you," the receptionist said, rushing forward to take the iPad from me.

"Oh, yeah. Thanks."

Okay, so if this was the doctor I was getting, I was happier to come to a place like this.

She gestured to the first room. "Right in here. I'm Dr. Martinez."

"Nice to meet you," I said, shaking her hand.

Axel and she exchanged pleasantries, and we were soon sitting in the small office, with brightly colored pictures on the walls and a bookcase behind the desk like one I always pictured I'd have in my dream home.

"What a great room," I said, glancing around. "I love it."

The doctor smiled at me. "Thanks. I love it too. So, tell me, how I can help you today."

Axel reached out for my hand and squeezed it, which I assumed was the signal for me to talk.

"Oh, okay. Well basically, I'm pregnant, which was a bit of a surprise. I have no idea what to do next or what to expect, so Axel said he'd find the best obstetrician for us, and here we are."

The doctor's grin was genuine. "Well, I appreciate the vote of confidence." She glanced down at the paperwork. "So, you'll be about six weeks according to your dates, but we can confirm that with a dating scan today. How are you feeling at the moment?"

"Terrible." I huffed out a laugh. "Nauseous, exhausted."

"Any vomiting?

"No," I said, "Not yet, anyway."

"That's good. Though you'll need to stay on top of your water content. Dehydration in early pregnancy is the main reason for hospitalization."

I picked up my bottle of water and took a big sip. "Thanks for the tip."

"I'll get you some pamphlets and information for your first trimester, then let's move into the next room to do your first scan."

We all stood up and the doctor opened a door into an exam room.

"Now this part looks like a hospital," I said, glancing around at the sterile white walls, the electronic monitors and equipment.

"Yes." She laughed. "This part is. Would you please wait in my office while we get ready, Axel?"

Axel glanced at me, and I nodded. "Sure."

He stepped out and she shut the door.

"This first scan is a little invasive. This wand goes inside the vagina, and then we can see the fetus and check for position and a heartbeat." She picked up a large metal rod, with a thick end and rounded cap, and applied a condom to it.

"Are you serious?" I asked. "You wanna put that thing inside me?"

She nodded. "Yes, it's the only way to see the fetus today. Unless you want to wait until twelve weeks for the scan. We'll order blood tests today to check your iron, vitamin D, pregnancy hormones, etcetera."

I stared at the thing she called a wand. "Is it going to hurt?"

"No. Just a little cold and uncomfortable."

I sighed. "Okay. I want to try it. I want to see the baby."

"Well, it's technically only a fetus, but I do find a lot of expectant mothers enjoy seeing this scan in particular."

"What do I do?"

She got me up on the table with no underwear on but draped under a sheet, then went and got Axel.

"Everything okay?" he asked when he walked back in.

I nodded. "Yeah, she'd going to do a scan to see the baby, then do blood tests and stuff. Do you have to get back?"

He shook his head. "No, I'm here as long as you need me."

I wasn't sure I believed him, since he seemed a little jumpy and had glanced at his phone three times already. But for the moment we were together, and this was important for him to be here for.

I reached out my hand and he grabbed for me. "Thanks for coming," I said, smiling up at me.

He ducked his head and kissed my lips, then pressed his forehead to mine. "Of course."

I closed my eyes, shutting out the bright lights and focusing on Axel's energy for the moment. Yes, this was the reason I was here, and in this position. My love for this man. It had been far too long since I'd felt his skin against mine.

"Okay, Chastity," the doctor instructed, getting my attention again. "Just put your feet on these little metal stirrups. It'll be a little cold and you'll feel some pressure."

"Oops!" I squeaked as she pressed a very wet, lubricated, cold rod into me.

"You okay?" Axel asked, looking concerned.

I shifted a little, trying to find a comfortable spot. "Yeah. Just a bit of a shock, really."

"Here we go. Just looking at this screen over here," Dr. Martinez said, adjusting a large screen to our left.

I stared at it, only making out weird black and white swirls.

"I can't see anything," I said, my stomach lurching with fear. What if I wasn't really pregnant? And I was just... I don't know, sick?

"There it is," the doctor said suddenly, moving the rod a little deeper and pressing harder.

"Where?"

She lifted her hand and pointed at the screen. "There. Now, I'll just measure it, and see where the heart is."

I watched her clicking on a mouse, amazed at the dexterity it took to do such a thing. Meanwhile, Axel was squeezing my hand tightly.

I glanced up at him. "You okay?"

He nodded, his eyes trained on the screen, not looking at me. "Yeah. Just can't believe this is really happening."

I laughed. "That's because you're not the one with a metal wand up inside you."

He glanced down at me then and pressed his lips together like he was trying not to laugh.

"Measuring six weeks and two days. Perfectly in line with your dates. And there—there's the heartbeat. Measuring at 160 beats per minute. Very healthy."

I stared at the screen and could suddenly see what she was talking about. A tiny little blob with a fluttering pulse that flickered on the screen.

"Wow." My eyes filled with tears. "That's our baby."

I glanced up at Axel, who was staring at the screen with wonder in his eyes that was mirrored in the love in my heart.

He kissed me again, this time harder. "I love you."

"I love you too."

The doctor took some images, organized the rest of the tests, and gave me enough info to weigh me down for the next month.

Despite the nausea and having some stranger stick a metal wand in very private places, I was having the best day of my life.

Chapter 19

Axel

THE NEXT MONTH FLEW BY. I WAS BURIED IN WORK BUT MANAGED TO get down to the apartment for a weekend in the middle of February. Chastity was constantly studying and feeling sick, so she was hard to get hold of sometimes, but we made do. Just.

We were both focused on the end goal. That she graduates, and I find a way to reduce my hours. Unfortunately, though, I wasn't holding up my end of the bargain so much.

I was sitting at my desk in the office late on a Friday night when Chastity rang.

"Hey, beautiful," I said, smiling for the first time today. "How are you feeling?"

"Ugh. Almost ten weeks today, and..." She groaned. "Wanna vomit every minute of every day. How are you?"

I frowned at the phone. "Are you drinking enough water?"

"Yeah, I am. Got a bottle next to me all day long. One good thing about feeling sick all the time though is I've lost five pounds. Worst diet ever."

"That doesn't sound good," I told her, worried at why she was weighing herself while pregnant. That didn't sound like a healthy thing to do. "Should we see Dr. Martinez a little earlier than planned?"

We had an appointment at twelve weeks, but I'm sure she'd get us in sooner if something was wrong.

"No, don't worry about it. It's totally normal, according to my app."

"If you say so." Maybe I should have been doing my own research, but I'd been buried in paperwork the last couple of weeks.

"Hey, how's the manager hunt going? Still no one you like?"

This was a question she asked once a week and unfortunately, I answered the same every time. "Not great. I interviewed a few people yesterday—"

"But they all sucked?"

I laughed, enjoying her quick wit and sense of humor. "Yeah, they all sucked. God, I miss you." And I did.

"Well, you could come down for the weekend. Have a night off."

I glanced around at my desk filled with everything I needed to have done by Monday morning. "I'm still at the office."

She sighed heavily. "So, you'll be working all weekend again."

My heart squeezed tightly. We could both use some time together and mentally, I needed a night off.

"How about I come down tomorrow night? I'll get a driver so I can use the time to work there and back, then take off the night and we can chill, have dinner. Whatever you want."

She gasped. "Really? Oh my God, I'd love that."

I laughed. "You're sounding better now."

"Oh, yeah. The nausea's even gone for the moment, I'm so excited. Thank you! What time?"

We discussed the details and said goodnight.

When I hung up, despite the extra burden I'd just laid on myself, I felt much happier. I'd never really understood those new-age hippy sayings about re-filling the well, and looking after yourself so you could look after others.

I'd always trained hard, eaten well, and run off my desire to succeed.

But it wasn't enough anymore.

I had another reason to work now, to breathe. That was Chastity and the baby coming. Without seeing her, all the stress and demands of work were becoming overwhelming.

I texted her a quick message as I smiled to myself.

Can't wait to see you and our secret little bump. Been too long. I love you.

Then I got back to work with a new enthusiasm. I worked all night, got four hours' sleep, then went to the gym in the morning.

When the driver came to pick me up, I was ready, packed and laptop in hand, prepared to work during the drive down. I hadn't thought about it before, as I liked driving my car and felt like a rich dickhead if I had a driver everywhere I went.

But this way, I didn't lose two hours of work time and could easily justify taking the night off. In fact, it meant that taking every Saturday night off was now possible. I could go down to the apartment, spend one night a week with my girl, and keep running my company.

The plan was in place. Now just to make sure it all went smoothly.

When the driver pulled up, Chastity's car was already parked out front but she was nowhere in sight.

"Thanks, Harry," I told the driver. "See you tomorrow around noon."

"See you then, Mr. Patterson."

I zipped up my briefcase, grabbed my bag and headed up to the apartment. My heart was light, and excitement buzzed through me.

When I opened the door, I called out, "Honey! I'm home." I sounded like some stupid sitcom character but it still made me happy.

Chastity called back, "Hi! Are you alone?"

I shut the door behind me and dropped my bags. "Of course. Why?"

Chastity walked out of the bedroom naked as the day she was born. "Just because," she said, shrugging like this was any other day.

I couldn't help it. I ran for her, picking her up and spinning her around, which she responded to by squealing and laughing. When I set her down, I didn't let her go, instead wrapping my arms around her warmth and tugging her close. "This is a nice surprise."

I glanced down at her glowing face, leaning back so I could cup her breasts and run my thumbs over her nipples. "These are darker than before." Her areolas, once a dark pink, were now browner in color.

She nodded. "Yeah, according to my app, it's a breast-feeding thing. They go darker so the baby can see them."

"Hmmm…" I loved that she knew everything about it, but it wasn't the focus for my sex-starved body at the moment. "So… does this mean I can take you to bed?"

She smiled coyly up at me. "Yes. I'm feeling better in the afternoons now, so I'd love to go back to bed for a bit."

"Oh, best news I've heard all day." I cupped her gorgeous face and kissed her, moaning when the pleasure of her lips against mine hit me.

Damn, I'd missed her. Her taste, her smell, her touch.

I swept my tongue into her mouth, kissing her deep, and long, and hard.

She grabbed me around the waist then started pulling at my shirt, getting her hands underneath and on my skin.

I groaned and pulled away, wanting to get as naked as she was. "Let's go." I grabbed her hand and pulled her into the bedroom, tugging at my clothes and throwing them to the floor.

"Anything I need to know?" I asked quickly, my hungry gaze roaming over her curvy figure. "Anything sore or sensitive?"

She bit her lip, her gaze running up and down my body. "Well, um… my nipples are a little sensitive, but everything else is good."

I fucking hoped so. My hormones were pumping now, and the weeks of missing her were adding up.

"Then get on that bed, missy."

Chastity turned and ran towards the bed, and I chased her, swatting at her round backside as she ran.

She jumped on the mattress and turned around, going down on her belly to face me.

"Uh?" Not sure what she was trying to achieve from that angle.

"Come here," she said, grabbing my thighs and hauling me closer.

When her wet, hot mouth closed around my cock, understanding clicked into place. "Oh, fuck."

A wave of sensation washed over me as she sucked on me, tonguing the tip and nibbling on the flesh that was so desperate to fuck her.

I grabbed at her hair and tugged her back gently. "Enough, or you'll make me blow right here." Her mouth was divine, but her pussy was heaven. And I'd missed the feeling of her wrapped around me.

She grinned up at me. "That wouldn't be a bad thing."

"Oh, yes it would. I want to make you come too."

I tugged her arm and gently pushed her toward the mattress, so she rolled onto her back. I slid over her luscious body, licking her nipples as I crawled up.

She wrapped her legs around my waist and whispered in my ear, "I'm so wet already. Please."

How was I going to say no to that?

Groaning, I shifted to line myself up with her. I rolled onto the side and took my cock in hand, dragging the head through her wetness and painting her pussy with her juices.

She gasped out her impatience, squeezing my arms. "Please hurry."

I met her gaze with my own and stared into her eyes as I rolled on top of her beautiful body. "I love you."

"Oh, I love you too." She wrapped her legs around me and tightened, urging me closer.

I felt her opening with my cock and thrust forward slowly, entering her heat and moaning as pleasure pulsed through me.

"Yesssss," Chastity groaned, throwing her head back into the pillows, her eyes closing on her own wave of pleasure.

I went slowly, even though it almost killed me. But I wanted her body to accept me, need me. Even get a little desperate for me.

So instead of fucking her into oblivion, hard and fast like my cock was demanding, I took it slow. For both of our sakes.

I rocked my hips, slowly going deeper and deeper. Penetrating her flesh again and again until Chastity dug her nails into my arms and tilted her hips up in greeting.

"Axel! Please! Stop torturing me."

That's all I needed to hear.

I drove in to the hilt, and we both cried out and how good it felt to be one again. Deep inside of her, I froze, needing the moment to get a hold of my control once more.

She dug her teeth into my shoulder, biting me softly. "Please don't stop."

"Oh, I won't," I ground out, finally ready to make us both fly to the stars.

I began to ride her harder and faster, chasing away the loneliness and time apart. Pounding into her wet, welcoming flesh until she was screaming my name. Until the room was filled with the sounds of the creaking bed frame and our sounds of pleasure.

When we reached the peak together, I thrust balls deep into her body and released my seed into her tight pussy. She rippled around me, squeezing my cock like a vise as her body shuddered beneath me.

I'd never felt anything like it. The pure, physical pleasure came through, then it was awash in love, in hope, in more feelings than I'd ever had to cope with before.

I rolled off her, so I didn't squash her and pulled her into my arms, holding her tight. I never wanted to leave this woman, which for me, was the scariest feeling of all.

Chapter 20

Chastity

WHEN AXEL ROLLED OFF ME AND TUGGED ME ONTO HIS CHEST, I WENT willingly. My body was totally satisfied and a little sore, so I closed my eyes to rest and enjoy the utter bliss that wrapped my body up in a cloud.

There was nothing like the post-orgasmic satiation feeling. Axel was an amazing lover.

I must have fallen asleep, because the next thing I knew, Axel was walking into the room fully dressed and I had my head on the pillow.

I blinked, wiping at drool falling out the side of my mouth.

"Oh… Ah…" I tried to speak, still exhausted and struggling to think. Shit, I felt terrible. Sick, weak.

I swallowed hard and forced myself to focus on talking. "Did I fall asleep?" I managed to ask, sitting up slowly, still naked, my stomach lurching.

"Yep. Sound asleep." He grinned. "Been an hour or so now and I thought you might want some dinner."

My head was a little weird, but I attempted a smile. "Yeah, sure."

"What's wrong?"

"Oh, I'm just a little dizzy. Probably hungry." Though the idea of food was making my stomach dip. "Actually, I might lie down again."

I put my head back on the pillow and pulled the sheet over my nakedness.

He sat down on the bed next to me and rested a hand on my hip. "How about I order in? Or I can go down the street and pick us up something?"

I smiled at Axel, so grateful that he was just so… him. "That sounds great. Hey, is it normal for billionaires to be so… well, amazing? And kind of normal at the same time?"

He cackled this time, then sobered quickly. "Ah, not really. Most of the men in my circle of business have yachts and helicopters. Full-time drivers and chefs."

Sounded like the perfect life… for some.

"Not you, though," I said, reaching for his leg and holding on to him.

I really loved that part about him.

"Not yet," he said with a wink, then stood up and walked towards the door. "I'm a bit starving so I'll go now and give you time to shower or rest, or whatever you need to do. You're looking a bit pale."

I swallowed hard. "Yeah. I get a few hours off in the afternoon when I feel okay, but the evenings can be rough."

I'd been so glad when Axel had recommended catching up around four pm. It was the only time of day I felt any good and we hadn't had sex in so long, I felt like a terrible girlfriend.

My body had missed it too. Wow! I'd come so much it had been amazing.

"I'll hurry. Back soon, beautiful." Then he disappeared.

I groaned, nausea rolling through me. The sickness had hit a real peak lately and I was hoping it wouldn't get much worse. I could barely think half the time and I'd almost failed a quiz recently. People at school were beginning to notice I wasn't myself, and I wasn't sure how much longer I could keep my pregnancy a secret.

"Shower time." I hauled myself to my feet and pressed a hand to my still flat stomach. "A couple more weeks and I get to see you on the screen again."

Everything I read told me that the sickness correlated with high pregnancy hormones and a healthy fetus, as a general rule. If that was true, then I had to hope and assume our little one was doing well. He or she had certainly taken enough out of me recently.

I staggered to the bathroom, still feeling dizzy but managing to have a quick shower before crawling back into bed. Nope. Wasn't going to be able to stay up much more tonight.

When Axel came back with food, I groaned a bit and he laughed. Which didn't make me feel great but lightened the mood considerably.

I ate what I could and fell asleep on him again watching a movie.

The next morning at breakfast, I managed to get up and go down to a cafe at street level, but I ordered a peppermint tea and nothing else.

"Are you sure you don't want anything to eat? You are looking a bit skinny," Axel said.

I would have laughed at the skinny comment if I wasn't feeling so sick.

I inhaled sharply, my nose practically twitching at the stench of cooked eggs and bacon around me. "Oh, no, I'm fine. The smell of the meat… it's just." I shook my head and swallowed the bile that rose.

I took a calming sip of my tea, then tried talking again. "The morning sickness is pretty bad at the moment, but it'll pass."

"When? Do you know?" he asked.

I sighed. "The books all say different things. Some women feel this sick all nine months, and if that happens, please shoot me."

Axel grinned but didn't say anything.

And I was only joking… sort of.

"Anyway, the general consensus seems to be that after twelve or thirteen weeks, it should get better."

He nodded and ate his Eggs Benedict, which seemed to be his breakfast of choice. "How are you coping with classes, feeling so ill."

"I'm not coping well," I told him, a little ashamed. "I'm trying my best, but I know people are noticing. My roommate, in particular."

"Does she know?"

I shook my head. "I haven't told her, but she's remarked on how pale I am. How much I sleep. Once we get the twelve-week scan done and I can tell everyone, I think I'll have to."

It was only a matter of time until my professors said something. "But I'm hoping I feel better by the end of the semester. I need to be okay for my final exams."

He reached over the table and squeezed my hand. "I'm sorry about the timing for you."

"Are you?" I asked, raising an eyebrow at him.

He grinned his gorgeous, flashy smile at me. "I'm not sorry you're pregnant. That's amazing and I can't wait to tell everyone I know that I'm going to be a father finally."

I squeezed his fingers, the excitement in his voice warming me all over. "I hadn't really thought about that. Have you always wanted kids but just didn't get around to it?"

He smiled and took his hand back so he could use both to eat. "Yes and no. I always said I wouldn't mind having kids with the right person, but to be honest, I wasn't sure that was ever going to happen."

"Which part? The kids part or the right person part?"

He laughed then took another bite of his eggs. "Well… both, I guess. I wasn't sure I'd ever find someone like you. And if I didn't do that, then I'd just work until I died, I guess."

He said it so matter-of-factly, I wasn't sure how to respond. "Um… well, I'm glad you did find me, and I'm glad you get to be a daddy."

His eyes flared at the mention of the word "daddy," but I didn't think he was thinking about the baby anymore.

"Is that an invitation to go back upstairs?" he asked.

Heat flushed up my cheeks and I buried my embarrassment by drinking some more tea. "Uh, sorry. No, I don't think I can."

Not unless he wanted me to vomit all over him. I could barely move at the moment without feeling sick. I couldn't imagine all the jostling that would take place if we were in bed.

He nodded, but I noticed the wave of disappointment crossing his features.

"I'm sorry."

He shook his head. "Don't be. I just miss you. That's all."

"I miss you, too. And if it wasn't for this—" I waved in the general region of my stomach. "—I'd be keeping you in bed all day and night like we used to."

He smiled, but the heat of his excitement was gone.

"I hadn't really thought about how difficult this must be for you," I said. "You've sort of lost your girlfriend, haven't you?"

I'd been so sick and focused on me, I hadn't really thought about how his life had changed.

"It's okay." He grinned. "You're doing an amazing job of growing our baby. That's all that's important."

"Thanks." I thought I was failing in lots of ways, especially at school. But his compliment was appreciated, nonetheless. I took a few more sips of tea and sighed. "Tell me more about why you're having so much trouble finding a manager."

When he looked away, I tried again. "I know you don't like to talk about it, but don't you think it's important that you take time off when the baby's born?"

"Of course, I do. I wouldn't miss it."

Wouldn't miss which part? The birth? The first few days, weeks? What about feeding? Nights? Was he going to help me at all?

"But who's going to run your company for you?" I asked, feeling a bit like a pushy wife. But this was important. "I want you around in those first few months, not just days. I'm going to need your help."

And surely, he'd want to be there for me.

"I'll find someone, Chastity," he said, his tone changing so that he was a little cold now. "And we can always hire a night nurse or a nanny. You'll have as much help as you want."

"I don't want a nanny," I said, though a voice in the back of my head said there might be a night I wanted the help. "I want you."

A muscle tightened in his jaw as he straightened up. "We have over six months until I need to take time off. So, please, stop harassing me about it. I'll find someone."

I gaped at him. "Harassing you? Excuse me? I'm just asking a question that you don't have an answer for."

He tugged on his shirt and frowned at me. "Leave it. My business has nothing to do with you. I said I'd sort it out, and I will."

Oh my God. Seriously?

"Fine." I finished my tea, and decided it was time to go back to school.

We said a frosty goodbye and Axel stayed in the apartment to do more work, waiting for his driver to arrive.

I drove the whole fifteen minutes home, seething the whole time. "Wouldn't want to miss a minute's work. After all, that is the most important thing in the world, isn't it?"

Maybe my dad had been right, and Axel was a workaholic who would never change.

There were worse things, of course. He wasn't into drugs or alcohol. He could provide for me and the baby, and if I never wanted to work, I didn't have to.

But I wasn't an ice queen.

I didn't want money, and no love or time.

It was probably unfair to want everything, but I did. I'd rather have to work and have a husband that was present than be one of those women who never saw her man.

I loved Axel too much to endure in silence, and I was going to fight for more.

Chapter 21

Axel

I'D THOUGHT AFTER OUR LITTLE SPAT AT BREAKFAST CHASTITY WOULD withdraw from me like so many other women had before her. The cold shoulder was a common game they liked to play. But she surprised me.

She called more often, messaged every day. It was almost like we were living together already. Almost. She'd ask about my day at work, then FaceTime me every night. She was completely in my life, and it was great. It was like having a full-time girlfriend, but because she was still in college and I didn't need to carve out time for dates, I didn't stop. Instead, I worked, non-stop.

Two weeks flew by and what felt like only days later, we were back at the hospital. I'd arrived early and met her here, and now we waited in a huge white room for the twelve-week scan.

Chastity's hand was on my thigh, and I sighed as I glanced at my watch. How much longer? I'd had to cancel two meetings and a lunch appointment for this time slot.

"The sonographer is running an hour or so behind, but she'll be as fast as she can," the receptionist told us.

"An hour?" I repeated. They had to be kidding me.

The receptionist nodded, giving me an apologetic smile, and dashing away to the desk again.

Shit! I ran a hand through my hair, frazzled. I better get on the phone to Cheryl and rearrange some more meetings.

"Do you want to go?" Chastity asked me from the chair to my left.

I twisted around. "Go? And miss it?" After she'd asked me to come and reminded me of the scheduled time three times?

She nodded. "Yeah. I know you have a ton to do. And an hour for you is what… another million dollars?"

She winked comically to show she was joking, but she wasn't far off the pace with that one.

I'd never worked out a monetary value to my time, as every hour we made money. I also paid hundreds of employees per hour, so it was possible some days I'd be in the red.

But she wasn't wrong in her calculations.

"No. It's okay. I'll sit here with you and chat," I said, though my cell phone vibrated in my pocket, drawing my attention away from her.

Chastity sighed. "I have to get some bloodwork done too. How about I ask if I can do that now? You can take your phone calls outside, and we can meet back here in an hour?"

Gratitude for this beautiful woman swept over me. "You're amazing. Thank you for understanding. I'll just be at the entrance to the hospital, so if you need me, just call, okay?"

She nodded and stood up. "Okay. And we're doing lunch after this?"

"Definitely." I couldn't lose too much more of the day, but we both needed to eat. "How's your stomach? Are you okay?"

Her smile was bright this time as she ran both hands over her still flat stomach. "It's a little queasy, but it's better."

"Fantastic." I dropped a quick kiss on her lips. "Thanks for this." And thank you to the universe for sending me such an understanding woman. I raced out the door to work.

It was lucky I did go out to take the next call, because one of my deals was close to collapsing, and the insurance company I'd hired to cover me on a new build was balking at my additions to the contract.

I juggled three different calls and was still on the phone when someone tapped me on the shoulder. I twirled around to see Chastity's furious face, her mouth pinched, and her cheeks slashed with red.

"Ah... Michael. I need to go. I'll call you back when I can." I hung up on my real estate agent and slid my cell into my pocket. "Are you okay, sweetheart?"

What had I missed?

She crossed her arms over her chest in an exaggerated move and glared at me. "No, actually, I'm not okay. My bloodwork made me vomit. I fucking hate needles."

"I didn't know that." I wasn't sure what I could have done to help her even if I had been there.

"And you've been gone almost two hours and wouldn't answer your phone."

Two hours. No way. That would mean I'd missed everything.

"What?" I pulled my cell out and glanced down at the time. "Oh, no."

"So, you missed the sonogram. Congratulations. You've proven my dad right. You only care about your work, and even a baby isn't going to change that."

That wasn't fair. Not in the slightest. "Chastity, be reasonable."

She picked up her bag, rummaged through it and came out with some small pieces of paper. "Here," she said as she slammed her hand into my chest.

I caught the soft paper that she pushed at me and stared down at the little black and white pictures. "Uh..."

"That's the baby," she said, crossing her arms once more. "Which you missed out on seeing with me, even though you promised me I wouldn't have to do this alone. That you'd be there for me."

I couldn't really see much except circles and smudges. I knew Chastity was connected to this more than me, but I really couldn't get excited the same way she was.

"Uh..." I looked back at Chastity. "I'm so sorry sweetheart. I didn't realize—"

"What? What didn't you realize? That this was important to me?

And I thought it was important to you too."

She was really angry. Her face had gone white now and I wasn't sure how to handle her. "No. I didn't realize so much time had gone by. Why didn't you call me?"

"I DID!" she screamed, her arms straightening as she tightened her hands into fists. "I called you three times and sent you like TEN MESSAGES."

Then she turned and stormed off down the street.

Oh. Fuck.

I ran after her, my Italian leather shoes really not made for hustling. "Wait! Sweetheart, please wait." I grabbed onto her arm and tugged her a little.

She stopped and whirled on me. "What do you want?"

Ah, whoa. I hadn't seen this side of her before.

"I thought we were going out to lunch afterwards. Please, let me make it up to you."

"You CAN'T make this up to me, and I don't WANT to have lunch with you," she all but hissed at me. "I'm going back to school. My plan was to tell my parents about the pregnancy after the scan, but now that I'm not sure about you and me and what we're going to do. So, I'll wait."

I froze, like someone had thrown a bucket of ice water down the back of my shirt. "Uh… sorry. Repeat that. I don't understand what you mean."

She couldn't be saying what it sounded like she was saying. Who broke up with the father of their baby over one missed doctor's appointment?

"I meeeeean," she said with exaggerated, teenager-like attitude, "that I don't know what sort of relationship we have, Axel. And I'm not going to tell my parents that I'm pregnant until I know how you and I are going to function as a family in the future."

My jaw dropped open. "You're not sure about us? All because I missed one appointment? You have to be kidding me."

She was joking, right? She had to be.

"I'm not kidding, Axel. I've tried to ignore your workaholic tendencies and the fact that you don't have room in your life for me. I convinced myself that you'd make space for me and for us in your life when the time came. But I'm not sure I can wait six months to see what sort of partner and father you'll be."

I stared at her, shocked. "Chastity, that is not fair. I give you every spare moment I have, every day."

"Exactly!" She exploded again. "You have two minutes here, and five minutes there. That's not a life, Axel."

"But I—"

"Have you hired a new manager yet? Or two or three or four? Because to make up for even half the hours you work, you're gonna need half a dozen guys, I'd say."

I straightened up, a wave of annoyance washing over me. "Chastity, I've spent fifteen years building my company. I can't just suddenly step back and hand off my roles and responsibilities to someone else. It doesn't work that way."

Her eyes filled with tears this time, and my heart all but broke. "Goodbye, Axel. Enjoy your billions."

She pushed past me and walked away.

I stared after her, totally conflicted as to what to do. So instead of acting on the impulse to chase after her once more, I just stood there like an idiot and watched her get into the car I gave her and drive away.

I was still standing there on the sidewalk, when my phone began to ring again. I grabbed for it, hoping and assuming it was Chastity. Had she changed her mind? Did she want to yell at me some more? I didn't care as long as she wanted to contact me again.

But it wasn't Chastity. It was Neil from the office.

"Ah, yeah," I responded to whatever he said. "I'm heading back now. I'll be there in fifteen minutes."

I wandered to where I'd parked the car and got in.

That's when I remembered the pictures, and pulled them out of the pocket I'd shoved them in.

Most of them were blurry and hard to decipher, but the last one was totally different. Some sort of 3D technology where I could actually see the baby's head and face, nose and mouth.

"Wow." It looked like a real baby already. Probably as small as an apricot, or something silly like that. Chastity had sent me a picture this morning describing how big it was.

I groaned and threw the pictures on the passenger seat, started the car and took off.

Just because I made a mistake, did not mean I was going to be a bad father. I knew a bunch of men who missed every appointment their wives made, and some of them missed the births too.

That didn't mean they didn't love their wives or their children.

Although once I thought about it, half of them were divorced now. Surely, their work ethic wasn't a factor in that?

It was simple statistics of marriage and divorce, that was all.

I shook my head, a stack of heavy emotions squeezing inside my chest. I had to work through this problem so I could find the best path forward. Chastity was very important to me, but she was being unreasonable.

Perhaps it was the hormones? Or stress and lack of sleep? I had to talk to Chastity again. Surely, she'd see sense when she calmed down again.

Chapter 22

Chastity

I'D NEVER BEEN SO ANGRY IN MY ENTIRE LIFE.

"That stupid… fucking… JACKASS!" I screamed to the inside of my new car. The car he'd bought me. "Fuck. Him."

The college was on the right of me as I drove, so I slowed down and pulled into the dorm's parking lot, then parked into the nearest spot on an angle and couldn't be bothered reversing to fix it.

I turned the engine off with a flick of my wrist, still shaking with fury, then slammed both hands into the steering wheel. "Fuuuccck!"

What an asshole. What sort of guy promises to attend the most important moment of our life, then walks outside to work on his phone for two hours? And worst of all, he didn't even notice how much time had passed!

I got out of the car, slammed the door, and stomped all the way back to my dorm.

Something could have been wrong with the baby. Did he even think about that when he left me? Abandoned me to my fate? Our fate, supposedly? Together.

Luckily or possibly unluckily—I wasn't sure yet—my roommate Hope was in our dorm room when I got back. She was studying quietly, her reading glasses on while she sat at her desk in the corner of the room.

I stormed in, slammed the door behind me and threw my bag on the bed with a scream of frustration.

Hope whirled around on her swivel chair and pulled off her glasses. "Hey! What happened?"

"That… that…" I put my hands on my hips and faced my room-mate. "I'm pregnant, and you may as well know, because the whole world is going to find out soon enough."

I'd start popping soon and there was no way I was going to be able to hide my belly, even in my graduation gown. Who had I been kidding when I made that joke?

Hope nodded slowly and bit her lip. "Yeah, I assumed so."

I gaped at her. "You already knew?" Wow. And I thought I'd done a good job of hiding it.

"Yeah, well… I guessed anyway. You're always feeling sick, you've lost weight, you barely eat." She shrugged. "I figured you were either pregnant or something really bad was happening to you. But it's been months, and I know you and Axel are pretty serious. So…"

I collapsed down and sat on the bed opposite her. "Why didn't you say anything?"

"Because it wasn't my business. And I knew you'd tell me when you were ready."

Love swelled in my heart for the girl I shared my room with. "Thank you for that." After the day I'd had it was nice to be pleasantly surprised about a person.

She grabbed her bottle of water and took a swig. "It's okay. I still feel bad about being a bitch about Axel. And I'm still really sorry about how I was at the start."

I sighed. "It's okay. You were probably right about him."

Hope got up and walked over to her bed, sitting on the mattress so she could face me. "Why? What's happened?"

I sighed. "How long have you got?"

"All day," she answered, staring at me with patience and under-standing.

"O-kay." I took a deep breath and began, telling her about the appointment and what had happened. "I feel bad in a way," I said, snorting at my own stupidity.

"Why would you feel bad?"

"Because I kinda set this up as a test." Full well knowing that he'd choose his work over me, and desperately hoping I'd be wrong. But I wasn't, and it was my own stupid fault for thinking he might have changed.

Hope frowned at me as though she didn't understand, and of course she didn't. She couldn't read minds and knew nothing about Axel.

I sighed, deciding to reveal all. "Axel is a workaholic, and it's one of the reasons my dad doesn't think we should be together. For me, I've always thought it was a good thing. He has a great work ethic and has massive success because of it. But that was only until I realized that the baby and I are going to come in second to his work if something doesn't change."

And even though he'd said things would change and that he *wanted* things to change, today had shown that if anything, he was busier than ever.

"Does he have managers or someone who can step up and take the reins?" Hope asked.

"That's exactly what he suggested initially. That he could step back and hire someone to take over, or at least help him. But anyone he's tried out hasn't worked and I think he's just too used to being in control. He's not going to be able to delegate and step away. And I don't know..." I shrugged.

I felt totally lost in this regard. If he couldn't trust anyone to help him, we had no hope of having a life together.

"So, hang on. Back it up a step. So how was this day a test?" Hope asked, moving to the edge of her bed.

"Well, I've tried to be extremely supportive and a good girlfriend over the last few weeks, but I made it super clear that for me, this was one of the most important scans of the whole pregnancy. This would tell us if the baby was alive and well, and afterwards, I could start telling people, including my parents."

Which I still hadn't done, and felt sick to my stomach about doing, especially now.

Hope snorted. "And he missed the appointment? How?"

"Well, they were running late so I gave him the out. I let him go outside to work, which was something I didn't want him to do but again, was trying to show him how supportive I was. But when they came to get me, I rang him three times, and texted him a dozen times, all of which he ignored and just kept working."

I still couldn't believe he'd missed all my messages. He was literally *on* his phone.

Hope lifted her legs and crossed them, now sitting on the bed like a genie. "Well, if he was on the phone, your calls probably went to voicemail."

That wasn't the point. The receptionist gave him a time, and he never once noticed he'd blown an hour past it. "But he knew I was inside, waiting for him. This was our moment to see the baby. To check everything was okay with her."

"Her?" Hope asked, sitting up suddenly. "You're having a girl?"

I clapped my hand over my mouth. Oh, shit. "I didn't mean to say that! Axel doesn't even know."

"Oh, that's so awesome!" Hope said, grinning from ear to ear.

Sadness swept over me, pushing away the last of the anger. "Yeah, I think so too. It's not certain. I got a blood test that can determine the sex and checks for abnormalities and I'll get those results in a few weeks. But the sonographer said that if they had to guess, they'd say eighty percent chance it's a girl."

Hope sighed. "So cool."

It was! A baby girl to adore. Pink walls and blankets, hair ribbons and beautiful dresses!

Tears gathered in my eyes, and I blinked them away. "Yeah, it is. And he missed it. The whole appointment. We hadn't even decided if we wanted to know what it was and I was so angry with him for not being there for me, I just said yes I wanted to know."

And despite being angry about Axel missing the appointment, I still felt a little guilty about going ahead with the question without asking him what he wanted to do.

Hope tucked her hair behind her ear and sighed. "Well, look. He's definitely a workaholic asshole, I'm totally with you on that one. But he loves you—you know he does. *I* know he does. Everything he's done for you so far has been amazing."

She had a point. The sex. The Vegas trip. The car. The phone calls. The jewelery.

I lifted my hand and stared down at the vintage-style Tiffany ring on my hand and sighed. "Yeah, but if he isn't there for me when I need him, what use is there of being together?"

Hope put both hands up as though saying "stop." "Um, hang on a minute. You're considering breaking up with him?"

"Um, well…" Was I? Maybe? I was certainly angry enough to do so!

"Despite all the love, money, and sex? Just because he missed one appointment?"

I jumped to my feet and glared at her. "It's not about the appointment! It's about the fact that his company is always more important than me, and I can't have that be our lives. Is he going to miss the birth because work calls? Or the baby's first birthday? No!" I shook my head and pressed both hands to my belly, "No. We deserve to be loved, and for me, that is quality time."

"Then I think you need to talk to him," Hope said, standing up and going over to her stash of candy and grabbing a bag of jellybeans. "Want some?"

I nodded and held out my hand. "Yeah, we do need to talk." But what did I say? Hey hon, how about you pull your head out of your ass and focus on what's important in life?

My phone began to ring and I picked it up, staring at the screen for too long. "It's him."

Rage filled me and I rejected the call with one push of the button. Then, for good measure, I blocked his number in the settings. "See how he likes it."

Hope laughed and I twisted around to stare at her. "What?"

"Um, no offense, but are you sure you're not over-reacting? I mean… you're usually the nice one, always giving people a second chance."

I shook my head. "Not this time. I need some space to think." And work out what the hell I was going to do now.

"Well, I suppose you have six months," Hope said, stuffing more candy in her mouth.

I stared at Hope, absorbing her words. I did have six months. That was a long time. Longer than we'd even been together. "You're right. I'm going to have a shower. I feel totally dirty after those tests. I swear they're always shoving something in me or taking something out of me. It's gross. Then I'm going to eat and study. Gotta catch up where I've been falling behind."

And that's exactly what I did. I ate a late lunch, went to the library and ignored all the good news I'd had today. And the bad. For the rest of the night, I just wanted to be a college student with nothing to worry about except exams.

I'd think about Axel in the morning.

Maybe.

Chapter 23

Axel

When I got back to the office, I scrolled through my cell phone while I was getting off the elevator and walking in the door. There it was, the evidence of what Chastity had been complaining about. Multiple voicemails she'd left for me, several missed calls, and lots of texts that I really didn't want to read.

"Shit."

I went to walk down the hallway to my office but instead stopped, looking for advice since I was in foreign territory.

I ran my hand through my hair, brushing it off my face and behind my ear. I needed a haircut. "Hey, Cheryl, I don't know if you know the answer, but is there a reason I wouldn't get these calls or notifications if I'm on the phone?"

I handed her my cell, and she took it. Her face was calm as she clicked and scrolled through. I wouldn't trust anyone else with such a personal object, but Cheryl had been with me since day one of my business. I owed her for part of its success. She ran the staff like the captain of a ship.

Cheryl glanced up at me after thirty seconds or so. "Can I walk you to your office, sir?"

Oh, it was that bad, was it? Another thing I appreciated about her was her tact. "Yes, of course."

I followed my bustling hen of a manager, who just looked at the staff that were loitering and they jumped back to work. When we got to my office, she opened the door and went inside.

I shook my head.

Uh-oh. She never comes inside.

I shut the door to my office and walked over to my desk. "What is it, Cheryl?"

"I…" She swallowed hard, tears in her eyes.

Now panic was setting in. "Seriously. What's wrong?"

She walked at me slowly, arms raised. I went on instinct and moved towards her too. Her arms went around me, and she hugged me tight. I closed my eyes and let her hug me, squeezing her back.

When she pulled away, I let her go quickly. Our very first hug in fifteen years. I was shocked. She pulled a tissue out of the box on my desk I kept there for clients and dabbed at her eyes.

Feeling slightly uncomfortable, but also surprisingly happy, I finally sat down in my chair and looked at her. "Are you going to explain?"

She nodded and straightened her spine, back in professional mode. "The hug was to say congratulations, you're going to be a father. I'm so proud of you, Axel. It's wonderful."

It was my turn to fight back the emotions. This woman was the closest thing to a maternal influence I had in my life. My own mother was little more than a stranger. And despite the fact I'd never acknowledged Cheryl's role in my life, her approval meant more than I could say.

"Thank you, Cheryl. That means a lot."

She smiled for a moment, then stepped forward and sat down in the chair opposite me. "That said, what the hell happened today that you missed the twelve-week sonogram? You know how important that one is, don't you?"

I wasn't sure that I did, but from the look on Cheryl's face, I'd fucked up by missing it. "Ah… I know it's important."

Cheryl snorted. "But you don't know why. Okay. It's the scan that shows embryo viability. If Chastity had miscarried, or there was something wrong, this is the scan that would have told her, and she would have needed your support."

I shifted in my chair. "But nothing is wrong. Right?"

She ignored my question and kept plowing on. "And what the hell were you doing outside the hospital working while Chastity needed you?"

Well, that was easy to explain. "The doctor was running an hour late and Chastity told me to go outside and work for an hour."

"And did you?"

I frowned. "Did I what?"

"Go outside and work for an hour?"

Um... "I did go outside, but I lost track of time. I was juggling three phone calls and must have missed the time."

Cheryl pursed her lips and gave me a sour expression. "From the looks of those messages, you missed it by a long shot."

"Well, I..." *Didn't mean it. Not at all.*

And of all the people in the world, Cheryl should know that about me. I couldn't count the number of times she had to order dinner in for me, or call me from her house to tell me to finish up and go home. Time flew by when I was busy.

She cut me off though, not allowing me to explain. "And to answer your original question, if you have two phone lines going on a cell phone, a third person can't get through. So, if you were juggling that many phone calls, poor Chastity had no hope of getting you. And as for the messages, you probably ignored all the notifications, because they would have buzzed like normal."

I glanced down, unable to look at Cheryl at the moment. I felt her disapproval radiating off her like lava.

"I was on the street, the traffic was loud, and—"

"Your excuses are not going to fly with that poor girl."

I flicked my gaze back up to Cheryl, who now sat cross legged with her arms crossed in my chair. Yeah, she was mad.

"Poor girl?" I repeated. "I've given her an apartment, a car, a house!

Trips, jewelry, insurance, and everything else I can think of to spoil her. So, I miss one appointment. One! How does that make me a bad person?"

Chastity was over-reacting and Cheryl was too.

Cheryl stood up and put her hands on my desk so she was staring straight at me. "Axel, you know I admire you. As a boss, you're the best. But there's a reason you've never kept a girlfriend around for more than a few months."

"Yeah, because none of them were the one."

"No. Because you're already married."

I blinked at her. "I'm what?"

She stood up again and gestured to the room around us. "You're married to this company. To your success. And I'm not sure you can have both."

I tidied some papers on my desk that didn't need tidying and grabbed a fountain pen so my hands had something to do. "You're gonna have to speak a bit plainer, Cheryl. I'm feeling dumb today."

She clasped her hands together in front of her. "Axel."

Even the sound of my first name on her lips sounded weird. Up until ten minutes ago, she'd never used it before.

"This girl is the right one for you. I knew it the first time I met her. She is honest and down to earth, and if you sold everything tomorrow and ended up with next to nothing, she'd still want to be with you."

I swallowed hard. "How do you know?"

"Because I know women, and I can tell you've got a good one there. Better than I thought you'd ever find, to be honest."

I couldn't help but laugh at that one. "Really? You thought I'd end up married to... who?"

Cheryl flicked a piece of lint off her blazer. "Oh, well, a gold digger for sure. But the level of bitchiness and narcissism was still up for debate."

My jaw dropped open. "Wow. I didn't know you thought so little of me."

She actually rolled her eyes this time. "I think very highly of you.

But as a wealthy man who envelopes himself in luxury, you were always surrounded in women attracted to you for your wealth."

She tilted her head suddenly. "Where did you meet little Miss Sunshine?"

I smiled at the new nickname. Suited Chastity down to a tee. "At the health club, actually. She was waiting in the foyer having a hot chocolate and I was just leaving."

Cheryl's eyes lit up with entertainment. "That kind of makes sense. She wouldn't have known how wealthy you were, and you would have seen a beautiful young woman who didn't fit in at your club, and that piqued your interest."

She nodded once as though her curiosity had been satisfied.

I pinched the bridge of my nose. "Okay… so, can I get back to work now?" Back to the one thing in my life that made sense.

Cheryl stared at me like I was stupid, her eyebrows jumping up her forehead. "Have you got a plan for getting her back?"

"What do you mean, getting her back?" I hadn't lost her.

Cheryl sighed and turned to walk out the door. "Okay, but don't come crying to me when she breaks up with you."

I threw my hands up in the air and groaned loudly. "Fine! Come back."

She sauntered back to the chair and sat down.

Okay, I'd play the game. I took a deep breath and forced myself to stay calm. "Why do you think she's going to break up with me?" No one else had ever broken up with me, ever. "I mean…"

Cheryl stared at me with wide eyes again. "You haven't read any of your messages, have you?"

"I didn't see them." And had been avoiding looking.

"Well, I think you'll find that she's pretty furious, and with all her pregnancy hormones, she'll be jumping to the worst-case scenario."

I groaned. "I knew her hormones were making her over-react."

Cheryl pressed her lips into a thin line. "Please tell me you didn't say anything to her."

"Uh…"

Cheryl shook her head. "You are such a man sometimes."

"I don't see how that's an insult." Although it sure as hell sounded like one.

"I'm going to move along because I've got a list a mile long today." She clapped her hands together and looked me in the eye. "Do you want this girl?"

I didn't like being treated like a child, and it pushed up against my pride. But I chomped down on my ego and said, "Yes. Of course, I do."

"Then apologize until you're sick of apologizing, then start sending flowers."

That sounded tedious but doable. "You think she's that mad?"

"Have you called her yet?"

I nodded. "I did in the car, but I think her phone's switched off." Which was the only reason my calls would go straight to voicemail.

Cheryl stood up. "Or she's blocked you. So, in that case, start apologizing, don't stop apologizing, and I'll call the talent recruiter today."

She walked towards the door and has got as far as opening it before I called out. "Hang on. What talent recruiter?"

She twisted to look at me, already half out the door. "You know the only way you're getting Chastity back is if you prove that you can be a good partner, a good father, and that means working less."

It didn't sound like a question but I nodded, nonetheless.

"Then I'm getting you some managers. It's time you stepped back, Axel, and let the twenty-five-year-olds take over. You were a hot-head back then, and I'll find you another just like it. Three, if I have to."

I opened my mouth to respond, then slammed it shut again. "Thank you, Cheryl."

"You're welcome, Mr. Patterson," she said, assuming her assistant role once more. "You deserve to have a life. You've worked hard enough to be where you are. Time to enjoy more time outside of these four walls."

I nodded. "You're right. Thanks."

Cheryl left and I was filled with the intense need to get in my car and find Chastity. Track her down at school and beg her to come back. I'd pay for another sonogram, and we could re-do the day properly.

But I didn't. I swiveled around in my chair and stared out the window, my office allowing me a one-hundred-and-eighty-degree view of the city and the buildings surrounding me.

Cheryl was right. I could apologize, yes, but the only way of actually showing Chastity that I intended to change my life was to truly change it. I'd told her that I wished to work forty hours a week, but did I really want to pull it back that much?

Maybe I could start taking weekends off unless there was an emergency or a deadline. That would change a lot of my lifestyle.

"Argh.... I don't know." I lay back in my chair and sighed. This wasn't how it was supposed to be, and the worst part was, I wanted to call Patrick and tell him. He'd give me good advice and lament on how different women and men could be.

But I couldn't do anything more than call him for a run.

Oh, yeah, I definitely wanted a run. But first, I turned the chair back around and picked up my phone. I listened to the two voicemails Chastity had left and read the messages she sent.

Her calls were frantic and became increasingly angry.

Her texts were the same. And beneath it all was an overwhelming disappointment that choked me. She'd really needed me today. Was the multi-million-dollar deal that I'd saved with an hour's worth of phone calls worth it?

Probably was, since it was her future I was building too.

I had to tell her. I had to explain. But how did I do that when she was so angry?

I'd do what Cheryl suggested. Apologize for disappointing her, then start working towards my goal of reducing my hours, as soon as I worked out what that goal was. How far could I step back before the deck of cards collapsed?

Chapter 24

Chastity

I HATED TO ADMIT IT, BUT AT FIRST I'D LOVED IGNORING AXEL. I blocked him on my phone so I didn't get any phone calls or texts, and it was bliss. I got a ton of work done and stood on the moral high ground long enough to feel too content in my heightened level of happiness.

That feeling lasted about twenty-four hours. Then I started to miss him. Like, really miss him. Which sucked, because he was in the wrong, and I should be mad at him for a hell of a lot longer than one day.

But the doubt had started to creep in, and the guilt at how I'd acted. After all, I'd been the one to send him outside. I should have told him to stay, made him hold my hand through the blood tests. Maybe communicated better how much I actually needed him.

I shook my head to try and clear the thoughts from my mind. I couldn't study while my brain whirled, and second-guessing myself in regard to Axel was absolutely doing my head in.

It was Friday night, another week done, another step closer to graduation.

"You hanging around here for the weekend?" Hope asked from her side of the room as she packed her bags for a rare trip home to see her parents for the weekend.

"Yeah. I don't have any plans." And I was feeling so much better now. A lot of my fatigue and sickness had gone. Not completely, but it was better enough that I could actually catch up on the studying I'd been missing out on.

"Axel still hasn't called?" she asked.

I grinned at her. "I still have him blocked, so I have no idea."

"If his calls are blocked, he can still leave voicemails."

I'd never blocked anyone before, so I didn't know the rules exactly. When I unblocked him eventually, would a flood of messages come rushing into my phone?

I inhaled deeply through my nose and rolled onto my side on my bed to face Hope. "Yeah. There's a few on there. I've been avoiding listening to them."

Hope laughed while zipping up her suitcase. "Why would you do that?"

"Because I know he'll be saying he's sorry, and I'm not ready to hear it." I sat up and reached for my cell, staring down at its blank screen. I didn't want to admit to Hope or anyone else that I missed seeing his missed calls and messages there.

"Well, I'm off. But if you need me, I'm only a couple of hours away."

I smiled at her. We'd become closer than ever in the last few days. "I know. And thanks."

I'd considered going to see my parents this weekend, but since I didn't know what I was going to tell them, I just gave them my normal excuse about needing to study. I hadn't seen them for a few months, and although I was keenly aware of it, my parents didn't seem to have noticed the lack of visits.

There was a knock on the door and Hope walked over to open it.

"A delivery for Chastity," an unfamiliar male voice said from behind the door.

"Thank you," Hope said, then turned around with a massive bunch of roses in her arms and an insane grin on her face. "Look who got flowers."

I rolled my eyes. "What a typical thing to do." But I couldn't stop myself from sitting up on the bed and reaching for them. "Is there a card?"

"Yeah, on top."

The flowers weren't just flowers. They were perfect, long stemmed, red roses. My favorites. "Thanks." I took the vase and stared down at the roses for a moment, absorbing their perfection before I set them down on my nightstand and reached for the card.

It was a hand-written card. "Interesting. It actually looks like he wrote this himself." This was no typed card done by the lady at the florist, but then again it could have been written by Cheryl for all I knew. I didn't actually know what his writing looked like.

I stared at the card and read it aloud. "Dear sweetheart, I am so sorry I disappointed you. I will make it up to you. Love, Axel."

I sighed as my chest squeezed tight, my heart cracking open a little. "How does he think he can make it up to me? It's impossible." Tears that I'd been fighting all week swam into my eyes and I blinked angrily, rubbing them away. "No. I'm not going to cry. I promised myself I wouldn't."

I was going to be strong, for me and my little girl.

"Are you okay?" Hope asked, hovering around my bed.

"Oh, yeah, of course. You go. See you on Sunday night."

Hope reached down and hugged me quickly. "Call me if you need someone to talk to."

I hiccupped up a laugh. "I might need to, since you're the only one that knows about everything."

I hadn't dared to tell my mom or dad about the fallout between Axel and me, which sucked. I needed advice and someone to vent to, and yet the two people I trusted most in this world didn't know about my pregnancy and didn't want me to be with Axel.

They'd tell me to break up with him or get rid of the baby, or a hundred wrong things I didn't want to hear. So, help wasn't going to be found in that corner.

I waved to Hope as she left and focused on the card. He was going to make it up to me, was he? Did he have a time machine?

I fell back onto the bed and sighed, still clinging to the card. Maybe I should listen to his voicemails? Or unblock him? I didn't have to answer, but at least I could see what he was messaging me.

That sounded sensible enough, so I reached for my cell phone and unblocked him. There wasn't a flood of texts or anything that came in, so I had to assume that if he'd sent anything, it was now lost in the ether.

I pushed my phone away and closed my eyes. This wasn't fair. It wasn't meant to be like this.

Get up. Stop being so pathetic.

I forced myself to stand up and stretch. It was time to get some dinner, and maybe have an early night. I hadn't been sleeping very well despite being totally exhausted.

I did exactly as I'd planned, and fell fast asleep before ten pm, the aroma of my roses filling my nose and giving me sweet dreams.

THE NEXT DAY I WOKE UP TO A TEXT ON MY PHONE.

I'm not sure if you're getting these messages but I wanted you to know how much I miss you. Your voice. Your kisses. Everything.

I clapped a hand over my mouth to stop the sob from rising.

He wasn't playing fair sending messages like that. I missed him too much to even think about the fact that he missed me too. But what was the point of a relationship if I didn't trust him and couldn't count on him?

I thrust my cell phone away and went and took a shower, marveling at how much better I was feeling. I put my hand down on my belly, noticing the slight swell going on. "Good morning, baby."

Happiness filled me to the brim. A baby with Axel's gorgeous eyes, fitness and brains would be a handful. I'd be super busy when he or she was older, that was for certain.

I sighed, got out of the shower, dried myself and got dressed.

A wave of nausea flowed over me, but this time it felt more like hunger than anything else. "Hmmm… breakfast today."

I hadn't eaten a proper breakfast in months, so this would be interesting.

I managed a piece of toast and some apple juice. A win for me.

Then I went back to my room to study rather than the library. I wanted to stare at my roses a little longer.

When there was a knock at the dorm room door, I jumped. "Come in," I called out, though my heart had begun to pound like I was running a marathon. Was it him?

"Hi, sweetie!" my mom called out as she stuck her head around the door.

"Mom!" I cried, jumping to my feet and racing for her.

She wrapped her arms around me, laughing as she hugged me tightly.

I couldn't let go of her once I had my arms around her. The tears rose and I sobbed, burying my head into her neck.

"Hey, hey, hey. What's going on?" Mom asked me, brushing back my hair off my face.

"I'm just so glad to see you," I sobbed, rushing for the tissue box to mop up the tears on my face and blow my nose.

"Oh, sweetie, I'm so sorry it's been so long."

Mom walked across the room and sat down on my bed. Then she grabbed my hand and tugged on me to sit down. "Come. Sit."

I blew my nose, tossed the tissue in the wastebasket beside my bed then grabbed another tissue in case I needed it. "What are you doing here?" I asked her. "Not that I'm not glad to see you. I am, obviously, but I wasn't expecting you."

Though I had the apartment to use if Mom wanted to stay overnight, which would be great.

"I know you weren't, but I just woke up this morning and felt like I had to come and see you. So, I grabbed a takeout coffee, and here I am."

I smiled at my mother, her instincts insanely on point. "Are you going to stay until tomorrow? We can go sleep at Axel's apartment tonight if you want. It's got three bedrooms."

Mom's cheeks colored as she blushed bright red. "Um… thanks, sweetie, but I have a date tonight, actually. Dinner at eight. I can stay most of the day, but should try to head off around four, so I've got time to get ready."

My jaw dropped open. "Really, Mom? Wow! That's great."

'You think so?" she asked, her tone so hopeful it broke my heart.

"Yes! Of course! You deserve to be happy." And she was so young still. Barely forty-three. She still had forty to fifty years of life ahead of her, And I wanted her to find someone to spend those years with.

"Who is it?" I asked. "Where'd you meet him?"

"Oh… well, maybe I should take you to brunch and tell you," She stood abruptly.

That didn't sound very good. "I just had breakfast, Mom." And there was no way I could eat any more without worrying about my morning sickness. "You can tell me. Hope's gone for the weekend, so you can relax."

But my mother was doing the complete opposite of relaxing. She was wringing her hands and pacing back and forth across my room.

I slid to the edge of my bed and narrowed my eyes at her. "Why are you acting so strangely, Mom?"

She ran her hands through her hair, looking the very picture of worried. "I came all this way to tell you the truth, but now that I'm here, I'm terrified."

I pushed myself up to my feet. "What is it, Mom? Quick, tell me before I think it's something terrible, or you're dating someone younger than me or something."

That would serve me right, wouldn't it? After all, Axel was the same age as my parents. Would it be the same if my mom was dating a twenty-year-old guy? I wasn't sure I could deal with it.

Mom stopped and twisted around to look at me. "It's your dad," she all but squeaked.

I crossed my arms over my breasts and leaned forward. I mustn't have heard her properly. "Uh… come again?"

"It's Patrick. We uh... went out for coffee a few months ago, just to, you know... talk about you. And it was nice. We had a good time. So, we had a dinner, and another dinner. And then—"

I raised both hands into the air and pushed them out at her as though to say stop. "Hang on a second. Let me get this straight. You're dating my father? After twenty years of being broken up, you two are together again?"

She nodded quickly, jerking her head up and down in too fast movement. "And there's something else."

She looked terrified now. Her face was pale and there were tears in her eyes.

I rushed over to her and took her hands in mine, totally blown away but wanting to push those feelings aside to help my mother through whatever this was. "What is it, Mom? Did you find him with someone else?"

She shook her head animatedly. "Oh, no, it's nothing like that."

I squeezed her hands. "Tell me. It's okay. I'll help you if I can."

She laughed and rolled her eyes heavenward, blinking quickly as if to stop the tears from flowing. It was a move I knew well. "No, it's not like that, I just..." She stopped again, and it was my turn to sigh.

What on earth could it be?

Chapter 25

Chastity

I stared at my mom, waiting impatiently for her to tell me whatever she'd come to say.

When she didn't start speaking, I moved my hand in a circular motion to tell her to get a move on and groaned in impatience. "Go on, Mom, I'm dying here. So you are Dad are dating again. That's good, right?"

She seemed happy about it. I was still processing it myself. They'd always been at odds, about pretty much everything. And I could feel an undercurrent of annoyance at the fact that they'd decided to make it work when I finally didn't need them to. It would have been nice for them to have sorted this out twenty years ago, but still.

Stop being so selfish.

Mom nodded, then bit her lip, still not speaking.

She was obviously stressed so it had to be something totally crazy. An idea occurred to me, and I grinned at her. "You two aren't getting married again?" I laughed. "Because that would be kind of weird."

They'd gotten married when Mom was four months pregnant with me, and were divorced before I was two years old. I wasn't sure how I felt about the idea of either of them marrying again, let alone marrying each other. *Weird* didn't even begin to cover it.

Mom gave a nervous giggle. "No, it's not that. Oh my God, I wish it was that."

It was worse than them getting married? "Now you have to tell me. Spill."

Mom tugged her hands out of mine and walked a few feet away, then twisted around to look at me. "I'm pregnant."

"You're… what?" I whispered. *No.* "You can't be."

It was impossible, she was old! And I was… no, no, no.

"I know, right?" my mother said, pressing her hands to her belly in a protective gesture I knew too well. "It's crazy, but I am."

She was grinning like a loon, like she was happy about it!

"How far along are you?" I whispered, wrapping my arms around my waist.

Oh God. Oh God. Oh God.

"Only about nine weeks, but I had to tell you!" Mom exclaimed, her face lighting up like she was announcing that money was falling from the clouds instead of rain. "Even though I know it's a little early to get my hopes up. I've been feeling so sick, and my doctor said my hormone levels are good."

Then she bit her lip and stared at me, worry clear in her eyes. "Are you really upset?"

"Well… uh…" I had no idea what to say. "I think I need to sit down." I staggered back towards my bed and sat down on the mattress once more. "Shit… uh…"

"I know what you're thinking," she said, beginning to pace once more.

I doubt that very much.

There was no way my mom knew I was thinking about the Father of the Bride Part 2 plot we were re-enacting. My mom couldn't be pregnant at the same time as me. She couldn't.

"You're thinking I'm way too old to be doing this," she said, throwing her hands around in that flamboyant, animated way she had. "I had to stop drinking, which was not fun, I can tell you. And going back to the start, when I'd just finished raising you. It's crazy. I know, I'm crazy."

You definitely are.

Mom practically bounced across the room and jumped on to the bed with me. "But I've always wanted you to have a baby brother or sister."

"Oh, well—"

"And I know you won't be around the same way you would have been when you were little, but I hope you'd still want to be a part of this baby's life. Because I want it, Chastity, I really do. And your dad—"

I jumped in, interrupting her for once. "How does he feel about it?"

"I only told him a few days ago. He's…" Mom shook her head but was smiling at the same time. "He's really happy, actually. Worried about me, but he can't wait. We both can't. This time will be different."

Famous last words.

I pushed the tornado of feelings down and focused on my mother. "What are you two gonna do? Move in together?"

What would they do? They both owned their places, but I wasn't sure who'd relinquish their home first. Dad, maybe? Mom's house would probably be better for the baby. More space.

"I think we will, probably," she answered, sounding uncertain. "We haven't decided how or where, but we've got time. Seven months, give or take."

Seven months. She had seven months to plan her future, and I had six months to plan mine.

The avalanche of emotions that I'd been pushing down began to leak out between the cracks. Tears blurred my vision and pain crushed my chest until I couldn't breathe.

"Oh, no. You're really upset! I'm so sorry, my darling girl." Mom hauled me into her for a massive hug.

I tried to hold back, but I couldn't. Three days of holding it all in and I couldn't stop the tears any longer. I curled into my mom and cried hard.

"I'm so sorry," she kept repeating, and I was too overwhelmed to tell her it wasn't her fault. So, I just let the emotions flow, crying and sobbing and clinging to my mom until the storm had subsided.

When I finally pulled away, I grabbed for my tissue box, grateful there were a few left so I could mop up the mess on my face. "Don't go anywhere," I told her, though my throat sounded rusty and the words cracked. "I need to wash my face."

I raced to the ensuite and splashed some cold water on my cheeks and around my eyes. I looked horrible now, red, blotchy and terrible. But I had to get back in there. Mom needed to know that I wasn't crying because she was pregnant. I probably would have cried with her here anyway. Her timing in lots of ways was kind of perfect. I needed to talk to her.

So once I felt a little more human, I straightened up and patted my face dry, then took some deep, calming breaths. I couldn't hide my news now, not anymore. She deserved to know the truth.

"I'm so sorry, Mom," I told her as I walked back into the room, grabbed my swivel chair from my desk and sat on it. "That wasn't about you. I have a lot going on at the moment, and I think your news was just the straw that broke the camel's back. So, thank you for letting me cry. I needed it."

I took another slow breath, feeling the emotion rise within me once more. Shit, I wasn't going to get through this conversation without crying again.

"So you're not upset?" she asked, her tone hopeful.

"No… not at all. I'm, surprised, of course. But if you're happy, Mom, how can I be anything but happy for you?"

"Oh, thank you, sweetheart!" Mom jumped up and moved to hug me again.

I put my hands up to stop her. "Wait, don't hug me just yet."

Mom stopped, midway, arms outstretched, and recoiled back to sit on the bed once again. "Well, okay. How come?"

"Because I have news for you too, and you might not be happy with me, so let's try and keep all the hugs for the end." Hopefully there would be hugs at the end. I had a terrible feeling there wouldn't be.

"What's happened?" she asked, her eyes wide and wary now.

I stood up and wandered over to the roses by my bed. "Well, shit…

I'm not even sure where to begin. Let's start with the shit news. Axel and I had a fight."

I wasn't looking at her. I couldn't, so I just stared into the endless perfection of his gift.

"Have you two broken up?"

I shook my head and spun around to look at her. "No, I don't think so. He keeps messaging to apologize, and he sent flowers, but I'm not ready to talk to him yet."

"What happened? Did he cheat on you?"

I gaped at her. "Oh my God, no! Why would you think that?"

"Oh, sorry. It's just Patrick said that Axel's always been kind of a player, and with you two doing the long-distance thing, I sort of assumed..."

I leaned back against the wall behind me and crossed my arms over my chest. "You assumed that because you don't know him, Mom. He wouldn't cheat on me. He's got more integrity than that."

If he wanted another woman, he'd just tell me. He wasn't the sort of man to lie and sneak around. I would put money on it.

"Is that the ring he got you?" Mom asked, pointing to my hand.

I put my arm out and wiggled my fingers to show her. "Yeah, that's it."

Mom took my hand and stared down at the rose gold creation nestled around my ring finger on my right hand.

She didn't say anything, so I explained, "He called it a promise ring."

Mom nodded. "Yes. That's beautiful, Chastity."

I could see she was totally overwhelmed by the size of the ring and chose to ignore her discomfort. I didn't want her making some comment about his money that I couldn't cope with right now.

"So, what happened?" Mom asked.

I sighed. "Basically, I wanted him to go with me somewhere important, he missed it because of work, and I'm mad at him for prioritizing his company over me."

Mom screwed up her face as though she wasn't impressed with my answer. "That's a bit unfair, Chastity."

Uh… excuse me? "You don't even know what he missed."

She narrowed her gaze at me. "You didn't tell me. But from what you've said so far, Axel works his ass off, buys you expensive gifts and trips, and calls every night and would never cheat on you. All in all, a perfect guy."

"But—"

"His success hasn't come from sitting around doing nothing all day, Chastity."

I rolled my eyes. "I know that, Mom."

"Would you prefer him to be unemployed? Or a student like you?"

"Yes, I think I would prefer it if he was a student," I told her, being a smart-ass out of spite.

Mom stood up and glared at me. "Then you need to break up with him, and go find yourself a nice, dumb, twenty-year-old. Because when you date someone twice your age, they have responsibilities you don't understand, Chastity."

"That's a bit much, Mom." How was she taking his side in this? She didn't even like him!

"You've never paid your own bills, sweetheart. So please don't tell me you know what it's like in the real world, because you don't."

I dropped my gaze, my cheeks burning with shame. "Gee, thanks."

"Look, sweetie, you know I'm not a real Axel fan. I think he's too old for you. But I don't think being mad at him because he missed a date or whatever due to work is a good enough reason to break up. If he was playing golf or drinking with his friends, that's a different story."

I wiped at the tears that had fallen from my eyes. "No. He was working."

She shrugged. "Then you're gonna have to choose. Do you want Axel, with all his workaholic tendencies? And the money that comes with it, I might add. Rings like that don't grow on trees. Or do you want a guy your age, who doesn't come with any of the money but none of the responsibilities, either. Because people don't change, Chastity."

I slammed my mouth shut and bit my tongue, figuratively, not literally. I personally thought people could change and my mom telling me to just get over it wasn't good enough.

She suddenly put a hand to her belly and staggered sideways a little. "Whoa, head rush. I think I need something to eat."

"Hang on. I've got something." I rushed to my nightstand and grabbed out my emergency supply of dry crackers and a bottle of water. I handed both to my mom, and she took them, munching on a cracker right away.

"Thanks," she said, sighing heavily. "You never made me this sick."

"So, you think it might be a boy this time?" I asked, pushing the conversation away from Axel and me for a minute.

"I don't know," Mom said. "But we'll find out soon enough. Because of my age, they're giving me every test under the sun."

"I can imagine." I glanced down at the ground. I knew a lot more about pregnancies than she was aware, so how to tell my mom that we were going to have babies at the same time?

I'd been worried that she wouldn't approve of me being so young or of Axel being the father, or me putting off chiropractic school, but this… wow, this was a whole new level of crazy.

Mom walked over to my headboard and stared down into my drawer. Then she scooped something up, more food I assumed, and turned around with a strange look on her face. "Chastity, what's this?"

I froze. There was my mother holding up the sonogram of her grandchild.

Chapter 26

Chastity

"Uh…" *Oh shit.* That was not the way I'd planned for my mother to find out about her grandchild.

"Chastity," my mother repeated, her voice harsh and clipped. "Is this yours?"

I nodded. "Yes. It's from the sonogram I had on Wednesday that Axel missed. That's why I'm still mad at him."

My mom groaned and threw the picture on the bed, placing one hand on her hip. "Well, shit, Chastity. This wasn't supposed to happen."

I gasped at her tone, so stark and harsh, almost cruel. And the way she'd disregarded the sonogram was just nasty. I'm sure she wouldn't have done such a thing to photos of her own baby.

Mom tsked again, shaking her head in disapproval like she used to when I was a child and she was scolding me. Like I'd come home late or failed a test.

I couldn't do anything but stop and stare at her. Her mouth was pinched like she'd sucked on a lemon, and it was obvious she was mad as hell.

Any other time I would have been falling over myself to apologize and fix whatever was wrong. I couldn't stand it when my mom was

161

mad at me. But today, after everything she'd just revealed to me, all I could do was think about how different her reaction to my pregnancy was in comparison to how I'd reacted to hers.

I bit my lip and tilted my head to the side. "Um… Hang on a minute, Mom. I don't think you're being very fair here."

"Fair?" Mom repeated, gaping at me. "You've known this guy, what? Four months? Five, maybe? And you haven't even graduated yet, let alone—" She gasped loudly. "Chiropractic school."

She slapped herself in the forehead with her palm, making a loud *thwacking* noise for effect. "You're going to have to defer. Oh, fucking hell, Chastity. This will really screw up your future if you go ahead with it."

"Go ahead with it?" I repeated, glaring at her. "I'm more than twelve weeks and my baby is healthy. I'm healthy! Why the hell would I choose not to continue with it?"

Mom put both hands on her hips. "Because it will ruin your future! Don't you see? You're just repeating my mistakes."

"Your mistakes?" I threw my hands up in the air. "Why am I always referred to as your mistake?"

I'd heard it since before I could remember. The guilt trips about everything she'd missed out on. And when I got to my teenage years, Mom would torment me with stories of how she got pregnant and all the reasons why teenagers having sex was a bad idea.

She was the real reason I'd still been a virgin at twenty-one. She'd terrified me from childhood. And despite all that, I was now in the exactly position she'd always said she didn't want for me. Her position —her life.

But I had one key difference. Axel.

Mom's eyes dimmed as she realized what she'd said and how I'd taken it.

"I didn't mean it like that," she defended, and my temper exploded.

"Oh, yes you did!" I bellowed at her, walking across to the other side of the room so I could put some distance between us. "You always fall back on that excuse. Blaming me because you didn't finish college and have struggled with your life. But it wasn't my fault that you got pregnant so early."

"I know that."

"And it wasn't my fault that you made Dad drop out of college to take care of you. That you two broke up."

She crossed her arms over her chest and pouted. "I know that too. But—"

"But nothing, Mom. This is different. I love Axel and he can take care of me financially, which is something you never had. I'll graduate from college even though I'll be twenty-five weeks pregnant, and if I never go on to the next level, then so be it. Axel said I never have to work again if I don't want to, and that's certainly not the life that you ever had."

I clenched my hands into fists at my sides, hot anger pouring through me.

"Chastity," Mom said, her eyebrows lowering into an angry frown. "You need to really think about this. A baby will tie you to Axel for the rest of your life. You don't know him well enough for that, and you're too young to realize what you're throwing away by having a baby this early."

"What are you talking about?" I screamed at her. "I know exactly what I'll be missing out on, because you've reminded me of it every day of my life. You didn't get to travel or graduate. Re-marry. Well, I'm not going to have any of those problems because Axel is rich. And he'll make sure we travel and enjoy the world. My life will be different than yours, and I can't believe you can't see it."

She didn't want to see it, I knew that. My mother was jealous as hell that I'd found such a wealthy boyfriend, for my first relationship. She probably wanted me to struggle along like she did. She said she wanted better for me, but I wasn't sure she really did.

"You're the one that can't see it," Mom hissed at me like a snake. "You're a baby yourself. You can't look after a child. You can't even cope with Axel missing one appointment because he was off making more money. You two will never make it and then you'll be stuck with a baby all by yourself."

She had that super smug look on her face that I hated. She always thought she knew better, and in this case, she couldn't be more wrong.

I took a breath, my anger exploding. "You came here to tell me you have a completely unplanned pregnancy at the age of forty-three, with your ex-husband whom you've barely spoken to in twenty years, and you have the gall to tell me it'll never work?"

Who the hell was she kidding? Was my dad kidding? They were never going to last. They didn't last time, and what had changed in twenty years? Nothing.

"Chastity," Mom said, turning her head slightly, giving me the side eye.

"No." I stomped to my bedroom door. She was not in the right here and I would not be talked down to today. Not over this. "You need to leave. But thank you for doing the one thing I needed you to do—put my relationship with Axel into perspective."

Mom rushed over to me and grabbed for my hands, but I shook her off. "You need to leave."

"But—"

"No buts. It's pretty obvious who needs a reality check around here, Mom. I have always supported you with whatever you needed to be happy. And today, when you needed me to support your life and your choices, I did. But you find out the exact same thing about me, that I'm pregnant to a man I love, and you fly off the handle and want me to get rid of it?"

Her bottom lip quivered a little. "That's not what I said."

No, she couldn't have said exactly that, could she? But I knew exactly what she'd been thinking, and it made me sick."

"Well, you said enough," I said to her. "Thanks for nothing."

Mom opened her mouth to argue again, and I groaned. "Fine. I'll leave then. Because I'm not hanging around here, waiting for you to go." She could drag this out for hours. According to my father, she'd been the queen of drama. I'd never really seen her in full flight, and I didn't intend to.

I stomped over to my cell phone, grabbed it, and ran out of the room. Then I dropped to a jog but kept moving down the hallway and out into the fresh air.

"Gahhh!" I screamed out.

Shit, I didn't grab my keys, which meant that I was stuck on campus. It would have been great to be able to jump in the car and just go. Put some distance between my mom and me.

I shook myself. No matter. There were a lot of places I could hide where she couldn't find me. I twisted on the ball of my feet and marched off in the direction of the library cafe. I needed a coffee.

Oops. Shit. I couldn't. No caffeine for me.

So, I just kept walking and stomping my feet until I found myself running out of steam.

Then a thought occurred to me. Who was the first person Mom was going call and bitch about me to? "Oh, shit. Dad!"

I didn't want my mom telling him about my pregnancy before I did. We'd always had a deal, Dad and me. That I wouldn't let him be blindsided by Mom about anything related to me. I'd had to text him under the cover of darkness multiple times just to give him a heads up on something she had planned.

And despite their relationship changing, I still felt like I needed to be the one to tell him if she hadn't done so already. I took out my cell and pushed the button to call him. Three rings in and with my stomach in knots, he picked up.

"Hey, Chastity! Long time, no talk."

Oh, good, she hasn't got to him yet. "Hey, Dad! I need to talk to you for a minute, can you spare the time?"

He grunted as though getting up from his chair. "Ah yeah, give me a minute. I'm just going to walk somewhere quite."

I waited, impatiently tapping my foot against the concrete and looking around. I half expected my mom to just jump out of nowhere and sabotage the phone call. Where would she be, anyway?

"Okay. What's up?"

Which one should I start with? His news or mine?

"Uh, Mom visited me this morning and gave me your good news."

Dad was silent for a minute then he said, "I didn't know she was going to see you, otherwise I would have come too."

"It's okay, Dad. I know you always try and do the right thing. That's why I'm calling you. I'm happy for you and Mom, I really am. You both deserve a second chance to be happy, and if this is it, then I couldn't be happier for the both of you."

"Thanks, Chastity. I wanted to tell you, but it seemed too early to say anything."

I nodded, tears welling in my eyes. "That's how I've been feeling lately too."

"What do you mean?"

"I have news for you as well. I thought it was too early to say anything up until this week, then I chickened out on telling you. But Mom knows now that she surprised me on campus, and she's angry at me, so I have to tell you now." *Even if you get angry at me too.*

"What is it?" he asked. "Are you okay?"

I laughed, swallowing the tears in my throat. "Um, not really. But that's just because Mom and I had a fight. Overall, yeah, I'm good." Except for the argument with Axel, but I was very quickly putting that in perspective.

Funny how a fight with my mother could make me realize I was being too harsh with Axel.

"Well, tell me," Dad urged.

I took a deep breath. Shit. I was going to have to call Axel and let him know that both my parents knew. After all, my father was practically in shooting distance of Axel in the city.

"I'm pregnant too," I said quickly. "Over twelve weeks. I had my scan on Wednesday, and everything is good. I've been wanting to tell you guys but haven't known how to say it because I knew you'd be disappointed in me. But I'm going to graduate and Axel is going to take care of us, so you don't have to worry about anything."

I finished the words all in a rush, and despite the fact Axel and I hadn't worked out our issues, I knew he'd look after us financially no matter what. He'd already given me a house, for cripes sake!

"Wow... I don't know what to say."

My heart sank and I staggered over to a park bench. "You can ask me how I'm feeling or what Axel thinks. Anything, Dad."

Just please don't tell me I'm throwing my life away. I didn't think I could handle going through that conversation with both of my parents in the same day.

"I don't know what to say," he said again, in the same bewildered, shocked tone.

I blinked and hot tears coursed down my cheeks.

"Okay, Dad. Bye."

"Chastity, wait—"

I hung up on him, my heart breaking. I'd known my parents weren't going to take this news well, but a small part of me had hoped, really hoped I was wrong. That they'd be happy for me, or at least ask if I was happy. Surely that was important. Wasn't it?

Dad tried to call back, but I just let it go to voicemail. I needed to call Axel now and let him know that both of my parents might be coming to berate him. My mom would have trouble with a two-hour drive ahead of her, but Dad, well, his work wasn't far from Axel's.

I picked up my cell phone, tears blurring my vision.

I couldn't call him because I'd just burst into tears, and no one wanted that. Instead, I send him my first text in three days.

Hey. Thank you for the roses. They're beautiful. We need to talk, but I can't at the moment. Sorry. Just told my parents about the baby and they were as supportive as anticipated. Just warning you. Talk soon. xox.

The air shuddered in my chest as I tried to breathe.

How had this day turned this badly so quickly?

My phone began to ring, and I stared down at the screen. Axel was trying to call me, but I'd just told him I couldn't talk. And I *really couldn't.* My throat felt swollen and sore.

I closed my eyes and shook my head. No. I couldn't talk to him. Not now. I was going to walk back to my room and go back to bed. Maybe if I woke up a second time all of this would just go away.

Chapter 27

Axel

I stared down at my cell phone. She'd rejected my call. Again. I shouldn't be surprised, but I was.

I sighed loudly and pushed it across my desk. I was a bit tired of the games, but what could I do? I was in the wrong this time and had to suck it up and wait for her to come to me.

My office phone rang and I picked it up. It was a Saturday, so I was only doing a half day.

"Yes?"

"Mr. Patterson, I have my lead candidate here to meet you."

"Send him in, Cheryl."

My office manager didn't work Saturdays much anymore, but she'd sworn not to stop working until we found a team of managers for me to start to train.

I wasn't ready to step down or slow down drastically, but Cheryl had convinced me that it was necessary for the benefit of the company and my relationship.

And I was sure once I was able to enjoy my weekends again, and slotted in a vacation or two, I might welcome the pull back. But for the minute, the fact I was being forced to change my work habits ate at me like a stomach ulcer.

The door opened and a woman walked in. First surprise. Not that I should be surprised by anything Cheryl did nowadays, she was a wonder, but I hadn't expected a female.

I stood up and walked around my desk to shake her hand. "Axel Patterson."

She shook my hand, meeting my gaze head on. "I'm Taylor. Taylor Maze."

"Nice to meet you, Miss Maze. Please take a seat."

She moved over to the chair opposite my desk and sat down, crossing her legs and placing her small black bag on the floor next to her chair.

"Please, call me Taylor."

"Then you can call me Axel. We're not very formal around here. Well, except for Cheryl, of course."

Taylor's eyes lit up as I mentioned Cheryl. "She's wonderful. You're really lucky to have such a brilliant office manager."

"Yes, I am."

Okay, so the girl before me obviously had the credentials I needed, or her resume wouldn't have made it past the first round of Cheryl's inspection.

Now I knew that Cheryl liked her, and the sentiment was mutual. That was rare, because Cheryl was tough. And she looked through you to your soul and judged you on it.

Which was why I trusted her, and why it made me happy that she liked Chastity.

"So, Taylor, tell me why you want to work sixty-to-eighty-hour weeks."

The money was always the allure for people, but that didn't mean they had the drive to do the job and be successful.

She smiled at me. "Because that's what you need to do to succeed. To buy a home in this city."

She was right, but I wanted a more in-depth answer.

"True. So, may I be frank?" I was starting to feel like this interview was redundant. She was a young, enthusiastic, qualified woman. Giving her a go at the job seemed like the right thing to do, and she couldn't do any worse than the last idiot I'd hired.

"Of course," she said, and sat poised, waiting for me.

I took a deep breath, getting ready to be more honest with a stranger than I was prepared to be with my own parents.

"The reason I'm slowing down, or at least trying to get more help around here at the executive level—" at my level, "—is because I've finally met a woman I want to spend my nights and weekends with. Go on vacation with. I've been working non-stop for two decades, and it's been pointed out to me that I deserve a life."

"You obviously do," Taylor agreed as she glanced around the room. "Look at all you've accomplished."

I'd hit all my financial targets, plus more. But the problem was the maintenance of such a huge company. All the moving parts needed constant attention, which was why a managerial team was the answer. Cheryl and Chastity were right.

The team could do the tasks I didn't enjoy, which would free me up to focus on new acquisitions and the clients who were too temperamental for anyone else to handle.

"So, tell me how you think you'll do being me—" I urged her, "—having your whole life revolve around work, because I have to warn you, you'll be here weekends, nights, early mornings. Not every day, but often."

I had to know if she knew what she was getting herself into. She was young, appearing about twenty-four, maybe twenty-five. She deserved a life too.

"I'm ready for that."

"Well, the last manager I hired told me the same thing, but the very first week I hired him, he took most of the weekend off even though there were meetings and deadlines to be met."

And he'd been motivated, according to him. Forty-five, and wanting to retire by fifty. I'd thought he was the perfect candidate.

But no, I'd been wrong.

Taylor shuffled forward on her chair. "May I be frank also?"

"Please," I said, gesturing openly to her. "It would be a welcome change."

The corporate world wasn't the place to find genuine, open people.

"I don't talk about my personal life generally with potential employers, but you seem to want to know the true reason I'm driven to work the way I do, so I'll tell you the full truth. I've been with my girlfriend for three years. She's a corporate lawyer and we live in a tiny apartment about two blocks from here."

I nodded. "It's good when you have a partner who has a similar drive."

Which I didn't have in Chastity, unfortunately. She didn't understand why I needed to work the hours I did.

"Yes, it is. But we sat down a few months ago and decided that we put aside ten years to work our absolute butts off, to buy a house. Travel. Get ahead. And then, if we wanted to, we would start a family. But I am absolutely committed to making our future a reality, so if you hire me, Mr. Patterson, I promise you will not regret it."

I stared at her and absorbed her passion. Many leaders talked about the "why" you need to keep working, keep doing whatever it is you're doing. For me, it had always been my parents that had driven me. I didn't want to rely on them for money, I wanted to impress them with my success.

It had never worked, but during the path to success, I'd found my true love for what I did.

Now, my "why" had changed, and yet I empathized with Taylor's position. And I found myself liking her also.

"You can start today," I told her. "With the caveat that you pass the drug screening and background checks. Of course."

She jumped to her feet. "Seriously? You don't want to know how many languages I speak? Or which college I went to?"

"Well, languages may be an advantage." I had several interpreters, but they weren't always available when I needed them.

"I'm fluent in French and can get by in most conversations in German and Italian."

She was perfect.

"I'll get Cheryl to bring in a laptop and you can work in here with me for the first few weeks, then we'll find you an office. Assuming, of course, that you don't quit before then."

"Oh, I won't, Mr. Patterson. Thank you." She reached over the desk and enthusiastically shook my hand.

"Axel," I reminded her.

She grinned. "Yes, sir."

"Well, let's get you started." I got my new manager a computer and off she went.

I ended up pulling a full day, ordering us takeout for dinner around ten pm and working until midnight.

When I woke up the next morning, I had hope that finding a proper management team was possible. And I had to tell Chastity.

I picked up my phone and it was only seven am. To text, or not to text. That was the question.

Screw it. I had to let her know.

Hey, beautiful. I'm hoping you want to chat today. I hired a new manager yesterday and she started work immediately. Call me when you can.

I sent off the text and I hadn't even stood up from my bed before she'd called.

"Good morning," I greeted her.

"Your new manager is a woman?"

I laughed at the obvious jealousy I heard in her tone. "Yeah, she's Cheryl's pick."

"Um… okay."

She sounded terrible. Depressed and lonely. I had to pull her out of the mood somehow. "She's only worked for me for one day, but I think you'll like her."

Chastity sighed. "I probably will. What's she like?"

"She's brilliant with numbers and convinced me she's driven enough to succeed, but we'll see. I've been fooled before."

"Is she married?" Chastity asked quietly.

I grinned. This was the cruncher. "She has a female partner, been together three years."

Silence.

"Oh, that's great." Chastity beamed now. "Can't wait to meet her."

Yeah, thought that might change everything.

"How are you doing, sweetheart? You've had a tough week, haven't you?"

She sniffed and didn't say anything.

My heart clenched. "I'm not sure how many of my messages you got, sweetheart, but please know that I'm sorry I missed the sonogram."

"It's okay," she said. "I shouldn't have over-reacted the way I did. I'm sorry too."

Whoa, that's a bit of a fast turnaround. "Um, although I appreciate what you're saying, what's happened to change your mind?" She sounded defeated. Not like my girl at all.

"I just… my mom pointed out that you weren't off drinking or gambling or golfing… can't remember. Anyway, she pointed out that you were working. And that's important, especially since I used the fact that you're successful against her when she was comparing our two situations."

"What situations?"

"The whole—oh my God. You don't know, do you? Can we FaceTime?"

Happiness exploded inside me. "Yes."

She hit some buttons and I sat back down on the bed and got comfortable.

Suddenly there she was. My girl. Looking a little pale, but better than I'd expected.

"I've missed you."

"I've missed you too," I told her. "Very much. So, what do you need to tell me?"

Her eyes went all wide and her mouth dropped open like a shocked cartoon character. "Guess what?"

"What?"

"Mom and Dad are pregnant again."

It was my turn to be stupefied. "Uh… excuse me?"

"Mom surprised me yesterday by driving up to school. She wanted to tell me she and dad have been seeing each other for a while, and that she's nine weeks pregnant."

"But… but," I stammered.

"I know, right?" she exclaimed. "I told her I was happy for them, but when she found my sonogram picture, she went off about me ruining my life and all this other crap that I'm so sick of hearing."

I shook my head. "That's insane."

"It is! Mom's forty-three."

"Yeah, God, I've gotta call Pat now." Would he be excited or angry that he'd accidentally impregnated the same woman twice?

She laughed then covered her mouth suddenly. "I talked to Dad yesterday and he wasn't very happy about our baby, so I hung up on him. I think I probably owe him an apology."

I jumped up off the mattress, struck with an idea. "How about I drive down for the day? I'll call a driver and be there around lunchtime. Do you have time this afternoon to catch up? I've missed you and that way I can apologize in person."

Her whole face lit up in a smile. "I'd love that. Meet you at the apartment? Or at one of the cafés?"

"How about we meet at Jenni's?" That was the breakfast café we liked the best. "I'll text you when I'm on my way, so you know what time to leave school."

"Sounds like a plan. Thank you."

"I'll call your dad on the way, find out if he hates me again."

Her eyes were big and watery as she nodded. "Yeah, give it ten minutes before you call. I've need to go apologize."

"It'll take me that long to line up a car and pack up. See you soon, beautiful."

I hung up the phone and raced to the bathroom, my heart thumping in my chest. I was excited to see her, more than I'd even imagined I would.

And Pat was going to have a baby too! Of all the crazy timing in the world.

My best friend and I were having kids together. And his son or daughter would be my son or daughter's aunt or uncle. Freaky.

Chapter 28

Axel

I WENT TO THE BATHROOM AND TOOK A SHOWER, JUST TO FILL IN THE time until I could call Patrick. Then I got dressed and put in an order for a car. I could work there and back and spend time with Chastity in the same day.

We had so much to talk about. But for now, Pat.

I glanced at the time. It had been twenty minutes since I spoke to Chastity. Surely, that was long enough for them to talk?

Hmmm... maybe not.

I made a quick protein shake with four eggs and kale, then packed for the day.

Then the driver arrived, and I jumped in with my laptop and cell. I sent off a text to Chastity to let her know I was on my way, then it was time to call Pat and find out how he felt about the burgeoning pregnancies.

The phone only rang once before Pat picked up. "I was just about to call you."

I grinned as the car wove through the city and relaxed back into my seat. "Chastity asked me to give her some time to speak to you. Did she call?"

"Uh, yeah. She did."

I rolled my eyes and scrubbed my fingers through my hair. "So, is everything okay with you two?"

There was a long silence then Pat said, "Yeah, she and I are fine. You and me, on the other hand…"

I stifled the groan that rose. "I wanted to tell you weeks ago, but Chastity asked me not to. She said she wanted to be the one to tell you."

More silence.

I pushed on, "I love her, Pat. And I'm really excited about the baby. I hope you can be happy for us too."

"You're gonna need to give me some time, Axel."

"For what?" I demanded, angry at my friend for being such an ass about everything. "I told you I love her, that I'll take care of her. I'd marry her if she wanted. If this was any other woman, you'd be happy for me. In fact, you'd probably say something like, 'Shit, this woman must be pretty amazing if you wanna commit like that. Wow. You a dad. I never thought I'd see the day.'"

Patty chuckled softly. "You're an asshole."

"Come on, man. Can you separate the two for a minute?"

There was a big sigh. "I can try."

"Fine," I huffed, then injected some happiness into my voice and pretended this was the first time my friend had heard the news. "Hey, Pat, guess what? I'm gonna be a father!"

"Congrats, buddy," Pat managed to say, though it was strained. "When's she due?"

"Early October."

There was silence again.

I cleared my throat. "Any news on your end?" I asked. "You know, with that woman you started seeing, and I didn't tell Chastity about?"

I coughed again to make the point. I hadn't told Chastity that her parents had started seeing each other again, which I hadn't liked doing, but did it for Patrick.

"Yeah, actually. I didn't think it would last past the first few dates, but it ended up being good."

"With your ex? That's surprising."

He huffed out a laugh. "Yeah, it has been. We… well, both of us have changed and grown a lot. But anyway, I have news too."

"Tell me."

Like I didn't already know.

Pat sighed. "Kaiti's pregnant. I'm going to be a father again."

"I want to say congratulations," I told him. "But you don't sound very happy about it."

He groaned. "Well, I—well… look. I am happy. It's just unexpected."

I laughed. "Is it too early to make a joke about the fact you've only knocked up a woman twice, and it was the same woman twenty-two years apart?"

I waited, holding my breath. But happily, part of my best friend was still inside my future father-in-law.

"Yeah, go for it. I've thought it a few times."

"You two obviously have good chemistry. What were the odds of her getting pregnant again?"

"At forty-three?" Pat asked. "The doctor said about one or two percent."

"Whoa. Sounds like fate."

Patty groaned. "You sound like Chastity. Stop it."

I grinned. "Hey, listen. I'm on my way to see Chastity now. I need to suck up for a mistake I made on Wednesday. Can we catch up tomorrow maybe? Dinner on me?"

"Do I wanna know what you did wrong?" my buddy asked.

"I missed her sonogram because I took some work calls."

Pat laughed. "I knew it. Your job is going to get in the way with you two."

"Shut up. I'm fixing it, okay?"

"Yeah, right. But okay, dinner tomorrow. I'll meet you at Jack's at eight?"

Jack's was our favorite steak place. "Yeah. Perfect. See you then."

I hung up feeling lighter and happier than I'd felt in months. Pat knew about our baby, Chastity wanted me down at the apartment to spend time together, and Cheryl was on the warpath to find me the best managers around.

Life was good.

ALMOST TWO HOURS LATER, WE PULLED UP OUTSIDE JENNI'S. I CLOSED my laptop and opened the door. "Hey, Terry, I should be ready to go by six pm."

"No problem, sir," the driver said. "I'll be here."

I got out and walked over to the café. I stopped outside and stared into the window. Chastity was sitting in a booth at the back, a cup of tea in hand.

Happiness filled my chest and I pushed open the front door.

She glanced up and her face lit up with a smile. I waved and forced myself to walk calmly across the room.

She didn't get up and jump at me like I was hoping, but she was smiling and moved slightly to the left so I could slide into the booth alongside her.

"Hey," I said, moving in and reaching for her.

She leaned forward and I kissed her lips, but she pulled back way before I wanted her to.

"Have you ordered?" I asked.

She shook her head. "No. Just the tea. It helps my stomach."

"How is the nausea?"

"Oh, so much better." She beamed. "The last few days I've been feeling much better."

"That's great."

The waitress came by, and we ordered drinks and food, then I turned back to my girl. "What can I do to make it up to you?"

She looked down at the table, gripping her mug tightly. "You can't."

"I'm very sorry, sweetheart. I didn't think about how my actions would affect you."

"It wasn't about the day. That appointment. Not really."

"What was it, then?" I asked, then thanked the waitress for my coffee, and went back to focusing on Chastity.

"It was what the appointment represented."

I sighed. Cheryl was right. "You think that I'll always prioritize work over you."

"Well, yeah. And I get it. I do. You've worked really hard to get where you are. With your company. And I admire your work ethic and devotion, but when it comes to the baby, I don't want an absent father."

Her eyes were welling up with tears as she spoke but she didn't let on, simply blinking them away.

Sadness swept over me.

"I wouldn't be absent."

She looked up and met my gaze and I could see the uncertainty swimming in her eyes.

"I wouldn't."

She sighed. "I suppose I need to just wait and see, but I need to say that if we stay together, I need a real partner. Not one that just earns money, throws a nanny at me, and pops his head into the kitchen once a week."

My jaw dropped open. "That's not what it would be like."

"I know, but—"

"Think about how much time we've spent together since we met. We've been on a weekend away, had a bunch of dinners and nights together. Hours on the phone almost every day."

I'd really tried with Chastity to have a normal relationship

"That's true, but we're not living together yet."

"I'd move you in today if I could, but you want to finish college first."

She sighed. "Only ten weeks to go."

"How's it going?"

She brushed her hand through the air. "I don't want to talk about school. Can we talk about what happens after I move in with you? How's it going to work?"

"What do you mean?" I asked. "Do you want to look at houses to move into together right away? I assumed we'd move into my apartment first, but you might have a point. We don't want to move too close to the birth."

She laughed. "That's, ah… not what I meant, although you're probably right. The apartment isn't the best place for a baby, but lots of people do it. I just… can we table that for later?"

I grinned at her, loving the terminology. "Okay. What did you mean then?"

"I mean, have you made any changes at work that will mean we can spend more time together? Or have you hired a housekeeper and a cook?"

The waitress brought our food and I stared down at my Southwestern omelet, suddenly ravenous. I picked up my knife and fork and began to cut.

"Well, I haven't looked into getting full time staff at home yet, but that's on the list."

It hadn't been on mine of course, but surely Cheryl would have it on hers, and that counted.

"Then what?" Chastity asked, picking up her fork and picking at her fruit salad.

"You've lost more weight," I told her.

She shrugged. "My appetite isn't great."

I made a mental note to talk to the obstetrician about that and continued on, "I've started making changes at work."

"Tell me," she said, looking excited.

"Well, the main thing, of course, is hiring my first manager, Taylor. But if Cheryl has her way, I'll have a team of them by the end of the quarter."

"Well, that's great," Chastity said. "But are you okay with that?"

"I'm worried about the company, it's true. But the way I was working isn't sustainable, so I'll start with one, then see how she does."

"I think it's great," Chastity said.

I thought about it for moment, then realized I felt the same way. "Me, too."

We both ate for a little while, then she asked, "So, I don't think you answered my question. What's going to happen next?"

"Well," I said, pushing my plate away. "If you'll let me, I'll take you upstairs and make love to you."

She glanced down. "Ah, maybe we can do that another time."

"Okay. Well, then how about a movie? A nap? What do you want to do?"

She chewed on her lip. "I just wanna talk for the moment."

"Sure. Should we get an ice cream or a hot drunk or something, and walk down the street?"

She nodded. "Yes, please. Some fresh air would be good too."

I paid the bill, grabbed her hand and tugged her into the street. I knew it would take time for her to wrap her head around everything and forgive me for disappointing her.

"Hey, you know I can't promise I'm always going to be perfect." I squeezed her hand as we walked along the street to the ice cream shop.

She turned to me. "Of course, I know that."

"But please understand that I'm going to try to be the best father I can possibly be." I wanted more for my kids than I had. Siblings, a proper home. Love and affection.

All the things that had been missing from my own childhood.

This time she beamed up at me with her huge smile. "I know. And I can't wait to see it."

Chapter 29

Chastity

I couldn't believe how nice it was to be back in Axel's company again. He was happy, and relaxed, and seemed totally ready to change things in his life for me and the baby. I keep wanting to pinch myself in case I was dreaming.

But were those changes even possible for a guy like him?

"Hey, can I ask you something?" I questioned after we'd gotten ice cream and were back walking along the sidewalk again. This strip of shops was quiet on a Sunday and it was nice to just be out in the fresh air and enjoying the sunshine.

"Of course."

"My mom and lots of other people have told me that a leopard can't change its spots."

He licked his own chocolate mint double scoop in a waffle cone and tilted his head. "Still waiting for the question."

Right.

"Well, your company is your whole life, right? How is it possible to change your priorities overnight?"

He grinned down at me. "Are you asking if I'm cured of my workaholic-ism?"

"I don't think that's a word." It didn't sound right, but I could be wrong.

He laughed. "Look, honestly, I don't know. I've worked my company up from just Cheryl and me in one office, to a building with more than a hundred staff. It's going to be hard to let go of a lot of the control. But if I want a life, then something's got to give."

Guilt hit me hard. Despite the fact that he'd done exactly as I asked, putting into place some steps that would make it easier for him to be a good father, I knew he'd done it under duress.

"I'm sorry," I said, glancing down at the ground.

Was I really *that* girlfriend? The one who made her boyfriend give up everything he loved to be with her?

That wasn't me. That *couldn't* be me.

"No, you don't need to be sorry," he reassured me, still walking casually along the street. "Hey, there's a nice little park right there. How about we sit and relax for a bit?"

"Yeah. Perfect," I said, stepping onto the grass and walking over to the little park bench. "Oh, that's better. Thanks."

My legs ached now, and I read online I needed to increase my magnesium or something. I had to get to a drugstore and buy some stuff when I had a minute.

Axel put his arm along the back of the seat, not around me directly, but it felt like he was hugging me in a strange way.

"I'm still sorry," I managed to say, because my appetite was gone and for the first time, I was beginning to see the situation from his perspective. "I didn't really think about how much you'd need to give up and change for this baby."

I'd been way more focused on what I was giving up.

"Hey, I told you that you don't need to be sorry. You are the woman I've dreamed of for so long. Someone I can truly love, and with a baby on the way, things couldn't be better. But it's true, I hadn't really thought about the other changes that would come with the dream."

I grimaced. "Yeah, me either."

"Are you coping with school? Is there anything I can do?"

I smiled, his offer warming my heart to him. "Thank you for saying that, but it's okay. I just have to put my head down and power through for a few months, then I'll be done and we can concentrate on the baby."

Axel grinned at me. "Do you want to talk about where we're going to live?"

I inhaled quickly, excitement filling me up. "Yes! What about that house that you gave me?"

It still sounded ridiculous to say out loud. He *gave* me a house, mortgage free. It was just an insane gift. Like winning the lottery, but the human kind.

"Oh, no, that's for you. For the baby."

"But I really liked it!" I continued. "Great location. Huge yard. Not too far from work for you." Not to mention the fact that the master bedroom had a jacuzzi in the ensuite.

He grinned at me. "If you like it that much, we can go see it on a free weekend. But that means you'll have to choose another house off the list because I want you to have something that earns money so you can invest it or save it for the baby."

I stared up at him, too much love in my heart. "You're incredible. Do you know that?"

He huffed and looked the other way, obviously not used to the compliment.

I twisted on the seat and reached for his right hand, holding it with both of mine. "I'm sorry I was so upset over the sonogram. Next time, I'll be more honest about how important it is to me. Or I'll get my mom to come or something."

Maybe.

He stared down at our entwined fingers, then up at me. "How is your mom doing?"

I sighed. "Not really sure. I haven't spoken to her since we had our fight yesterday."

She hadn't messaged once or tried to call, which was unusual for her.

"What happened exactly?"

I gave him a quick rundown on our fight, ending with me running off on her. Childish, I knew, But, God, had my temper been up yesterday. Then, as soon as she'd gone, I'd crashed, climbing into bed and not surfacing until the next day when Axel had messaged me.

I knew pregnancy messed with your emotions, but I wasn't used to the roller coaster of it all. Flaming furious one minute, in tears the next.

"What happened when you went back to your room?" he asked.

That had been a little strange. "She was gone. But the baby's picture was back in my drawer and it was shut, so she went to the trouble to clean up the room."

"Or she wanted to look at the sonogram again. I know I have been."

"You did? Then ones I threw at you?" I asked him, tears blurring my vision. I sniffed and blinked to force them back. "Sorry."

He grinned at me, reached into his wallet and pulled out my favorite of the sonogram photos. "I take it everywhere with me now. I'm not quite sure what I'm looking at, so I definitely can't miss the next appointment. I need a professional to show me what is what."

I laughed at him. "Yeah, it looks like a bit of a blur, doesn't it? Well, this is the head." I pointed to the large, round object in the picture. "This is the nose, and the little hand."

The tears were coming at me again. "I love looking at these pictures. I can't wait to see them in real life."

I so wanted to tell Axel about the baby's sex, but since it wasn't a hundred percent yet and he'd missed the sonogram, I decided to wait.

"I get my blood test results next week."

"What are they for?" he asked, putting his photos and his wallet away.

"They check my health stats like iron levels and vitamin D. But they also did a chromosome screening to test for abnormalities, and it will give us the sex of the baby."

His face went from interested to shocked, his mouth dropping open. "They can tell already? Isn't it a bit early?"

I laughed. "Yeah, I thought so too. But the new technology lets us find out relatively early." I swallowed hard, finding the need to lie uncomfortable. Should I tell him that I knew? "Um… the sonographer told me what they think the baby is. They said it's not a definite and to wait for the blood test results, but do you want to know what she said?"

Axel's face flashed with a myriad of emotions. "I'm not sure I want to know."

"Oh. Well, they were probably wrong anyway." Though the sonographer had seemed pretty certain, I didn't want to tell Axel that.

He suddenly jumped to his feet. "But you know and now I want to know because you know."

I pressed my lips together so I didn't laugh out loud. "I'll tell you, but you can't get your hopes up in case it's wrong."

He stepped away a little, then walked back. "How long before the blood test results?"

"They said a week, so by Wednesday, hopefully." I wanted the results so I could absolutely reassure myself that everything was fine with the little one.

He sat down again next to me and this time he put his arm around me properly. "I can wait a few more days then."

"Awesome." I put my head down on his shoulder and just enjoyed being with him. No phones ringing, no classes, no nausea.

I closed my eyes then yawned.

Axel chuckled. "You sure you don't want that nap? I'd love to just hold you for a while before I go home."

I lifted my head and stared up at him. My sex drive was extremely low at the moment, especially after the roller coaster of emotions I'd been through lately.

But just being with him? Being held by him? That was something that might chase away the depression that had been pulling me down into a hole the past twenty-four hours.

"That would be really nice."

"Let's go, then." Axel held out his hand, tugged me to my feet, then walked me back to the apartment building.

"I wasn't sure I'd ever come back here," I said to him as we walked into our bedroom, and he turned back the blankets.

"Why?" he asked.

"Well, I suppose I wasn't sure if we were going to make it, so I thought I may never see this place again."

Axel frowned at me. "Just because I made a mistake and we had a fight, that doesn't mean we're done. Please know that. I'll work through practically any problem with you."

It was exactly what I needed to hear. "Well, you are my first real relationship. I guess I kind of jumped straight off the deep end, and I'm sorry for that."

"It's okay." He grinned. "I've got a bit more experience with this stuff, so maybe I can guide you a little."

He unbuttoned his shirt and tugged the tails out of his jeans.

My mouth watered at the sight of him as more and more golden skin was revealed.

His shirt disappeared. Then his jeans.

I stared. I couldn't help it. He was so beautiful.

"Are we still just napping?" Axel asked, quirking an eyebrow at me.

I knelt on the bed and crawled across the mattress towards him. Maybe it was the fact we hadn't been together for ages. Or the fact that we were officially, definitely still together.

Maybe it was the fact that he was a gorgeous specimen of a man, and my femininity didn't have a chance at fighting the lust that passed over me.

I didn't know and I didn't care. I wanted him.

I reached the other side of the bed and knelt in front of him.

He quirked an eyebrow. "Are you sure?"

I nodded and reached out for him. "Kiss me. Please."

He groaned as he surged forward, cupping my face and pressing his lips to mine. I moaned with relief. We were finally together again.

He pushed me back, but I had too many clothes on to lie down. "Hang on." I slid off the mattress and got rid of my leggings and t-shirt, bra and panties.

Finally free of all the layers and warmth against my over-heated flesh, I jumped at him, kissing him, touching him. Wanting him on me, in me, all over me.

We fell in a heap on the bed, and I opened my legs for him. "Please. Just, now."

I wrapped my legs around him and he surged against me. I kissed his lips, moaning as I felt the head of his cock nudge my entrance.

More. I wanted more.

I flexed my hips up, taking him inside me. It stretched me, but I didn't want him to stop. I dug my nails into his back and as he pulled away, I gripped him and tugged him toward me.

He started off slowly, kissing me and rocking inside of me. My body relaxed, then he began to move faster, harder. Thrusting me into the bed, filling my body with his.

Again and again, I screamed out, wanting him, needing him.

All the angst of the week was washing over me, making me so grateful for this moment. That we were back together.

My stomach began to tighten and tremble. I closed my eyes and focused on the pleasure centered between my legs.

Axel dropped his head and whispered into my ear, "I love you. I love you so much."

And his words sent me soaring into the stratosphere and beyond.

Chapter 30

Axel

Chastity fell asleep after our session, and I held her for hours. There was no way I could sleep. My head was a whirl with possibilities and hope.

She loved me, and our baby was strong and healthy. Would it be a boy or a girl? Which one did I want, anyway?

When no answer immediately came forth, I realized I actually didn't care. Lots of men wanted a boy, a man to carry on the family name and to take to football practice.

But for me, as someone who wasn't sure I'd ever have my own child, either would be amazing. Though I did hope to have at least two. Growing up as an only child hadn't been fun, and I hoped Chastity felt the same way.

Eventually she stirred, moaning softly and lifting her head from my chest.

"Hello, sleepyhead," I said, kissing the top of her hair.

"Mmm… hey." She rolled onto her back and stretched her arms over her hair, affording me an awesome view of her gorgeous, darkened nipples and fleshy breasts.

"You've lost weight, but these look bigger," I said, running my fingers over her nipples gently.

She rolled onto her side and faced me. "Yeah, they are. I think I'm up two cup sizes already."

I rolled onto my side to face her as well. "Are you planning on breast feeding?"

"Yeah, of course." she said, then bit her lip. "I mean, as long as I can. I don't know much about it yet."

I leaned forward and kissed her lips. "We have time to learn, and whatever specialist you want to talk to, just say the word."

Her cheeks blushed pink. "Thanks."

"Hey, I know its early to even ask this, but how do you feel about a bigger family?"

"How big are we talking?" she asked with a grin.

I laughed. "Not ten or anything. But I hated growing up as an only child, so I suppose at least two. Just so they have at least one playmate."

Her eyes shone with happiness as she stared back at me. "Oh, at least two. I always hoped I'd have four, actually. Because I hated being an only child too. It sucked, big time."

I leaned forward and kissed her again, loving the feel of her warmth on my mouth.

Then I pulled back. "Let's start with two and see how we're doing." I had a lot of friends who'd assumed they wanted a whole tribe of kids, only to find out that two was more than enough.

My phone began to buzz so I grabbed for it where it lay on the nightstand. It was the driver.

I picked up my phone and answered, "Yeah, I'll be down in fifteen. Thanks."

I hung up and stared back at Chastity. "I'm sorry, I have to go. If I didn't have some international meetings online tonight, I'd stay."

She sat up and slid off the bed. "It's totally fine. I appreciate you coming all this way just for a few hours."

She ran off towards the bathroom and I watched her gorgeous ass as she went, then she shut the door.

I sighed, wanting to stay. I didn't want to spend two hours in a car working, to then work all night as well.

"Wow," I muttered to myself. "You are changing."

I laughed and shook my head, then forced myself to get dressed. I'd never really thought I'd find anything as important as my company and my goals.

When she walked back out still completely naked, I couldn't help myself. I rushed straight over to her and grabbed her up in my arms. "Damn, you're beautiful."

She laughed and grabbed for me, squeezing me tightly. "I'm going to miss you."

I pulled back, making an instant decision. "I'll come back next weekend, okay? You probably shouldn't be traveling too much with all your studies, so how about I commit to coming up here every weekend until graduation?"

Her jaw dropped.. "You'd do that?"

"Of course." I nodded my head. I'd make sure I could. "Unless you decide you want to come to the city to visit friends or whatever, and then I'll send a driver for you, okay?"

She nodded, her eyes filling with tears. "That would be great. I think it's going to get harder to be apart now."

I pulled her into me and hugged her close. "I agree. So, I'll be back next weekend, I promise. And hopefully I'll have another new manager hired, and I won't need to fire him for being incompetent."

She giggled as she pulled back, wiping her nose. "I bet you're a tough taskmaster at work."

I nodded my head. "Only way to be successful, especially at the executive level."

She cupped my jaw for a moment then went and grabbed her clothes. I should have been packing to leave, but I watched as her delicious body disappeared from sight.

Once she was done, I grabbed my clothes, packed my stuff, and took her hand. "I have to go, but I'll call you tomorrow. Okay?"

She nodded. "I'll walk down with you. I need to get back to my dorm. Exams to study for."

We walked down together, and even though every part of me was saying I should stay and luxuriate in her body and her love some more, I got in the car, and we drove away.

❧

AXEL

The start of the week went well. Taylor, the new manager Cheryl had hired, was a gun at finance and numbers and had already taken over two of my major accounts.

I'd interviewed two other managers from Cheryl's list but hadn't clicked with either of them.

It was Wednesday morning, the day we got our IPSI test results that Taylor turned to me. "Can I ask a slightly off-topic question?"

"Of course," I said, not looking up from my computer.

"Are you still looking for managers?"

"Yes. I need at least three more I think, to make it possible for me to take off the time I need in October."

"Are you going away?"

Oh. I hadn't told anyone.

I turned towards her, but she seemed to take in my mood and instantly apologized. "I'm sorry. I just realized that's a personal question."

Well, Pat and Kaiti knew. I had yet to call my parents but would do that after the results came in today.

"No. It's okay. We're starting to tell people. My girlfriend is pregnant and she's due in October. I've promised her I'll take some time off after the birth."

Taylor nodded. "Congratulations."

"Is there a reason you were asking?"

She nodded and twisted around in her chair to look straight at me. "Yes, well... I was hoping I could help you there. I was in an incredible class at Yale, and several of the people who graduated in the same year from there aren't happy with their current positions. We had a social event Friday night and so many of them aren't being used to their full potential. If you wanted some recommendations, I could easily tell you who is best suited for which department."

I hadn't even thought about Taylor's contacts.

"That would be great, actually. I'll make a list of what I need, and you book them in around the calendar."

Taylor grinned at me. "Done."

Then she got back to her work and the weight on my shoulders felt instantly lighter. If Taylor could create a team of highly talented, trainable people, then she could save my family life in one fell swoop.

My phone rang around lunchtime, and I grabbed for it. "It's Chastity," I told Taylor. "Would you excuse us?"

"Of course," she said, grabbing her bag. "I'll go get some lunch now."

I picked up the phone. "Hey, sweetheart, how's your day going?"

"Good," she said, all happiness and sunshine in her voice. "How's your day going?"

"Well, it's good, actually. Taylor, my new manager, just told me she knows several people from grad school might fit in here, so she'd going to set up some interviews for the team."

"She sounds great," Chastity said, and although there wasn't the jealousy from before, I knew she wasn't too happy.

"You'll really like her," I told Chastity. "Maybe when we're settled, we can invite her and her partner over to our place?"

"Oh, I'd love that!" Chastity beamed. "They're around my age, aren't they?"

I laughed. "Yeah, I didn't check her resume, but I'd say she's twenty-five or six."

Chastity huffed. "Better than a sixty-year-old like those guys at dinner."

I leaned back in my chair and grinned to myself. "You're right. So, tell me, have you got the results of the blood test?"

"Yes! That's why I'm calling."

I waited, but she didn't say anything else.

"Well?" I pushed. "What does it say?"

"The baby's healthy. No chromosome abnormalities or anything like that, which is such a relief."

"That's great," I said, feeling her relief wash over me. "And you? How were your vitamin levels and things?"

"Oh, I need some iron supplements, but that's okay. I can get them over the counter at any drug store."

"And?" I said, wanting to know the rest of the results.

"And what?" she asked.

I groaned. "Does it tell us the sex of the baby?"

She laughed. "It does. Do you want to know?"

Hmmmm. "I do, now that you know."

"I can keep it to myself if you want the surprise."

I wasn't sure about that. "I'm not sure that's possible. You'll buy blue paint or a pink blanket, and the surprise will go out the window."

"Well, it does mean we can prepare the nursery and buy clothes and blankets and things."

I ran my hand through my hair. "Maybe you should tell me this weekend when I see you."

"We can do that," she said. "I can buy a gender reveal cake or something."

"What's that?"

"It's when you ask a baker to make a cake and ice it so you can't see the inside color, but when you cut it open, you see the pink or blue cake."

I didn't think that was very me.

"Oh, or I've seen online people do balloons, or lights, or all sorts of different things.

"Forget it. Tell me," I said. I wasn't into those games or stupid party gimmicks.

"You sure?"

"Yes! This is our baby. Tell me what we're having so we can plan accordingly." And it may make me feel more connected to the little black and white smudge on the screen once it had a name and an identity.

"We're having a girl," she whispered.

"A girl?" I repeated. "Did you say we're having a girl?"

"Yes. Are you happy?"

Wonder filled me. *A baby girl.* "Yes, I am," I told her, swallowing the lump in my throat. "A baby with your smile, Chastity, will be the most beautiful thing in the world to me."

She squealed a little bit. "I'm so glad, because I'm so happy too! I can't wait to paint her nursery and buy her cute little things. Is it okay if I tell my parents?"

"Of course," I said. "We should take them out for dinner together and celebrate."

"Oh, yeah. Thank you. When Mom and I have sorted our shit, I'll organize it."

"Okay, sweetheart."

Chastity went on about all things pink and girly, but I couldn't keep up. My heart was full.

I was going to be a dad.

A girl dad. Nothing had ever been so perfect.

www.ingramcontent.com/pod-product-compliance
Lightning Source LLC
Chambersburg PA
CBHW062309200726
48292CB00004BA/1438